BARCELONA DREAMING

ALSO BY RUPERT THOMSON

FICTION

NVK

Never Anyone But You

Katherine Carlyle

Secrecy

Death of a Murderer

Divided Kingdom

The Book of Revelation

Soft

The Insult

Air and Fire

The Five Gates of Hell

Dreams of Leaving

NONFICTION

This Party's Got to Stop

BARCELONA *dreaming*

Rupert Thomson

CORSAIR

First published in the US in 2021 by Other Press
First published in the UK in 2021 by Corsair

3 5 7 9 10 8 6 4 2

A CIP catalogue record for this book
is available from the British Library.

HB ISBN: 978-1-4721-5354-8
TPB ISBN: 978-1-4721-5353-1

Printed and bound in Great Britain by Clays Ltd, Elcograf S.p.A.

Papers used by Corsair are from well-managed forests
and other responsible sources.

Corsair
An imprint of
Little, Brown Book Group
Carmelite House
50 Victoria Embankment
London EC4Y 0DZ

An Hachette UK Company
www.hachette.co.uk

www.littlebrown.co.uk

TO

Olga Jubany Baucells

AND

Giles Gurney

You used to be alright
What happened

—RADIOHEAD

THE GIANT OF SARRIÀ

When I was twenty-one, I fell in love with Pol. I moved to Barcelona to be close to him, and we married soon after. Within a year of our wedding I was pregnant, but things had already started to go wrong between us, and by the time our daughter was six months old we had split up and were living apart. Though I was from the North of England, I stayed on in Barcelona. I couldn't bear to leave. The quality of the light first thing in the morning, so bright and clear that the buildings seemed to have black edges. The green parrots that flashed from one palm tree to another. Long walks in the Collserola in April, to gather wild asparagus, or in September, to hunt for mushrooms. The beach every weekend in the summer, the mountains in the winter—and restaurants and bars that stayed open all night. It was a city whose pleasures were simple and constant—and it was a good place to raise a child.

For the first few years, I taught at an international school in Pedralbes, but I'd always dreamed of running a business of my own. It wasn't until my daughter, Mar, was in her early teens that I had the money—I came into a small inheritance—and not long afterwards I found a commercial property that I thought might work: two rooms and a backyard in Sarrià, an ancient, well-heeled area in the upper reaches of the city. I called the shop Trinket. The cheekiness of the word appealed to me. Though English, it had a Catalan ring to it. That abruptness at the end. The sudden, final consonant. When I first saw the name printed in gold script on the crimson banner that would hang outside, it perfectly described the kind of place I'd had in mind—an Aladdin's cave of unexpected and exotic treasures.

Mar decided to go to university in England. She wanted to explore her English roots, she said. By then I'd been running Trinket for five years. I wasn't making much of a profit, but I got by, and during her second year at Bristol I moved to a new apartment only a few minutes' walk from the shop. Both the main bedroom and the living room had sliding glass doors that gave onto an east-facing terrace, where there was enough room for a Marquesa plant, a small lemon tree, and several pots of red geraniums. Directly beneath me was an underground car park, with frosted-glass slats high on the back wall that were left open all year-round. If I was sitting in my living room with no TV or music on, I would hear car engines starting, or people talking on their phones. Once, a man cleared his throat, and I thought for a moment that there was someone else in the apartment. At first, this was all a bit unnerving. In time, though, I adjusted. Like the shudder of the fridge or the distant grinding of the lift, the noises even began to reassure me.

I had been living there for about eighteen months when I was woken in the night by the sound of someone crying. It seemed to be coming from below. I eased out of bed and stepped onto the terrace. It was a stifling, humid night in late July, and I could smell the jasmine that sprawled over the side wall of the building that stood opposite. Beneath it, as always in the summer, was the stale, slightly medieval smell of drains. The crying was quieter now, and yet persistent, as if the misery ran deep. It sounded more like a man, I thought, than a woman. Back inside, I pulled on a denim skirt and a T-shirt, then I picked up my keys and left the apartment.

When I reached the entrance to the car park, I felt a shiver of apprehension, but I shook it off and started down the concrete slope. At the bottom was a kind of cabin or kiosk. The man on duty most nights was a melancholy Venezuelan called Hector. He almost always brought his Alsatian, Rocky, to work with him. For companionship, he told me, rather than security. After all, Sarrià wasn't exactly dangerous. I peered through the window. On the desk were a Styrofoam cup of coffee, still half-full, and a copy of *Mundo Deportivo*. There was no sign of Hector. Perhaps he had heard the crying himself, and had gone off to investigate. Or perhaps he had taken Rocky for a walk. There was a special sandy area for dogs about three hundred meters away, on the other side of Avinguda Foix.

I moved on, into the car park. The walls were dark blue to waist height and cream above, and the air smelled of spilled oil.

"Hello?" I called out. "Is anybody there?"

The stillness of the cars seemed temporary, as if they were living things, holding their breath. Some fifty yards away, there was another slope that dipped down to a lower level. I doubted I would have heard the crying if it had come from there.

Then, just as I was thinking of turning back, I saw him. He was bent over a Range Rover, his forearms resting on the bonnet, his face concealed. He looked young. Nineteen, perhaps. Or twenty. When I stopped nearby, he lifted his head and looked at me. His face was wet, though he was no longer crying.

I spoke to him in Spanish. "Are you all right?" Then I said the same thing again, in English.

Wiping his eyes on the inside of his wrist, he glanced beyond me warily, as if he suspected I might not be alone. He was wearing a dark-red short-sleeved shirt and a pair of jeans that looked new. Something told me he had made an effort that evening. He had dressed up to go out.

"Do you need help?" I asked.

He looked at me and spoke in French, his voice subdued, no more than a murmur. I had studied French at school, but it wasn't a language I knew well. I had only a few basic phrases.

"Est-ce que je peux vous aider?"

He looked at his feet.

"Viens avec moi." I took him gently by the arm and guided him back through the car park, towards the ramp that led up to the street. "Mon appartement," I said. "Ce n'est pas loin."

He muttered something I didn't catch. Where was he from? North Africa, I thought. Probably Morocco. The city was full of Moroccans. People often complained there were too many.

On our way out, we passed the lighted kiosk, but Hector and Rocky hadn't returned. I'd let go of the young man's arm, and he was walking beside me. I noticed that he moved awkwardly. If he was in pain, though, he seemed determined not to show it.

As we reached the top of the slope, I remembered the French word for "hurt." I turned to him and said, "Vous êtes blessé?"

He threw me another wary look, then stared straight ahead. I chose not to pursue it.

Once we had rounded the corner, I pointed to my building. "Ici."

I hadn't yet worked out what I was going to do with him. I hadn't thought that far ahead. I imagined he would sit at my kitchen table and drink—a glass of water or a cup of tea. It would be a quiet place, where he could recover. If he wanted to talk, I would listen. If not, I wouldn't press him. Later, when he felt better, I would call him a taxi.

I opened the door to my apartment and he followed me, but he stopped just inside and stood with his back against the wall.

"It's all right," I said.

He asked where the bathroom was. I showed him. As he disappeared inside, I noticed a dark stain on the back of his jeans, as if he had sat on something wet.

The minutes passed, and he failed to emerge. I filled the electric kettle and switched it on. The clock on the oven said 2:47. When the kettle had boiled, I made a pot of mint tea and took it over to the table, then I fetched two cups, some brown sugar, and a spoon. There was still no sign of him. I went and knocked on the bathroom door.

"Ça va?" I said.

"Oui," I heard him say. "Ça va."

When he came out, we sat at the table and I poured the tea. He helped himself to two spoonfuls of sugar and stirred quickly, deftly, tapping the spoon twice on the rim of the cup before placing it back on the saucer. Without looking at me, he lifted the cup and blew across the top, ruffling the surface of the tea. He took a sip, then put the cup down. He performed each separate action with a kind of authority that made him seem both older and younger than he was. It was like watching a child pretending to be a grown-up, something I had often seen my daughter do. But these were clearly actions he had repeated so many times that they had become ingrained, and he appeared to find them consoling—they returned him to himself, perhaps—and it was only then that I began to wonder what he had been doing in a car park at two in the morning, and why he had been crying.

Once he had finished his tea, which he drank without saying a word—this silence also felt normal, learned—I asked how he was feeling. He nodded, but didn't speak. I told him it was late. I had to work in the morning, and I needed sleep. Rising from the table, he thanked me for the tea. I walked him out of my apartment and through the small lobby. On the street I gave him a twenty-euro note, which was all I had on me. For a taxi, I said. He took the money and stared at it. I asked if it was enough. Still looking at the money, he nodded again. I pointed along the street to the main road at the end. He could find a taxi on Avinguda Foix, I told him. They came down from the Ronda all the time.

"Vous pouvez me montrer," he said.

He seemed insistent, and also commanding, and though I was tired it felt easier to do as he asked. We walked to the main road without talking. The narrow streets were deserted, with metal blinds lowered on most of the small businesses and shops. We saw no one.

As we approached Avinguda Foix, a taxi drifted towards us with its green light on. Relieved, I stuck out a hand. The taxi drew up next to me, and the young man opened the door and climbed in. When the driver saw I had stayed on the pavement, he glanced at the young man in his rearview mirror, though his words were directed at me.

"Has he got money?"

I said he had.

The young man looked at me through the half-open window. "Merci."

The taxi pulled away. Its taillights glowed briefly, then dimmed, as it dropped down the hill towards Diagonal. Now the road was quiet again, I felt guilty for having turned him away. Couldn't I have offered him my sofa for the night? I walked back to my apartment, wondering if I had failed some kind of test.

THE NEXT MORNING, before opening my shop, I arranged to have coffee with my best friend, Montse. Montse was editor-in-chief at a small literary publishing house, and her husband, Jaume, taught at the university and wrote articles for *El País* and *Letras Libres*. I had met Montse in the nineties, at the gates of the international school Mar attended. One of Montse's daughters was in the same class.

When I arrived at the café, she was sitting at a table under the trees in her Jackie O sunglasses and a green linen jacket. Her long brown hair was pinned up. I ordered a *café con leche*, then told her what had happened a few hours earlier.

"Fucking hell, darling," she said. "You invited a total stranger into your apartment in the middle of the night?"

I was unable to keep from smiling. You could always rely on Montse for an extravagant reaction.

"I can't believe you did that," she went on.

"You wouldn't have done it?"

"Are you kidding?"

"He was in trouble. He needed help." Something made me want to go further, to widen the gap between us. "Actually, I think I could have done more."

"You did plenty." Montse shook a cigarette out of the packet on the table, lit it, and blew the smoke sideways, into the square. "What kind of trouble?"

"I don't know. I didn't ask." I decided not to mention the wet patch on the back of the young man's jeans. I'm not sure why. Perhaps I felt he wouldn't want the information shared.

"Was he good-looking?"

"Montse," I said, laughing.

"Well? Was he?"

"He was half my age."

"You didn't answer the question."

I looked past her, at the facade of the town hall. Green shutters clattered open on the third floor of the building next door, and an elderly woman stood in the open window, her face raised to the sun.

"If you want to know the truth," I said, "I've never seen anyone quite so beautiful."

Lowering my eyes, I stared at the bright silver surface of the table, not because I was surprised or embarrassed by what I had just told Montse, but because it was the first time I'd put what I had felt into words. When I saw the young man leaning against the Range Rover, I had been struck by his physical grace—the slenderness of his forearm, the curve of his back under his shirt—and when he lifted his head and looked at me the breath had caught in my throat.

I looked up. Montse was still gazing at me, her mouth tilting in a kind of smile, her cigarette alight but temporarily forgotten between her fingers. Then she remembered it. Seeing it had burned down to the filter, she gave a murmur of irritation and stabbed it into the ashtray.

"Well," I said, "you asked."

I was laughing again. You didn't often see Montse at a loss for words.

Business was slow that day. Sometimes a whole hour went by without anybody walking into the shop. When I finished making an inventory of the stock that had just come in—soap manufactured in Menorca, Breton glassware, jewelry from Sulawesi—I began to rearrange the window display, but all I could see was the young man in the car park, in his short-sleeved shirt and his new jeans. I couldn't imagine what his life had been like before I found him, or what it had been like since. Did he have family in Barcelona? Where did he live? What did he do for money?

That evening, when I got home, I called Xavi, a friend who was a sociology professor at the university. I asked about the Moroccan community, and he supplied me with some facts. Of the twenty thousand Moroccans living in the city, he said, a quarter were probably undocumented. The figures were only rough estimates, since many of the people in question hadn't applied for NIE numbers. They worked in the service industries, as dishwashers, office cleaners, and maids, or as fruit and vegetable pickers, or else they were involved in the black market. You must have seen the young men on Las Ramblas at night, Xavi said, selling cans of beer to tourists or handing out fliers for restaurants and clubs. Like immigrants everywhere in Europe, they were responsible for more than their fair share of crime, but that was only to be expected. They felt marginalized, and were the object of racism and discrimination.

"Where do they live?" I asked.

"Some live downtown," Xavi said, "in Ciutat Vell, Sants-Montjuïc, or the Raval. Others live in the northeast of the city—suburbs like Nou Barris or Sant Andreu." He paused. "Why the sudden interest, Amy?"

"Oh," I said, "no reason."

THE SOUND OF THE YOUNG MAN crying had woken me in the early hours of Thursday morning. The following Tuesday, when I came home from work, I found him waiting outside my building. Even though he was some distance away, I knew it was him. It was partly his body language, the way he was leaning against the wall, but he was also wearing the same shirt, the dark-red one with the short sleeves. Was it the only decent shirt he owned, or had he put it on deliberately, to make himself more recognizable? At that moment he turned his head my way and noticed me. He pushed away from the wall and crossed the road. He had a plastic carrier bag in one hand.

When I reached him, he greeted me in Spanish.

"I didn't know you spoke *castellano*," I said.

He shrugged. "Only a little."

I smiled. "I'm sure it's better than my French."

"No," he said, remaining serious. "Your French is okay."

Your French is okay. He hadn't said my French was good, as most people would have done. That would have been a lie. I admired his candor. With someone like him, you might have a chance of knowing where you stood.

I asked him how he was feeling. Better, he said. He had been to a doctor, in the Raval.

"A doctor?" I said.

He looked past me, towards Major de Sarrià. Dusk was falling, the deep blue of the sky edging into black. I hadn't been exaggerating about his looks—if anything, he was more beautiful than I remembered—and I felt something open or unfold inside me, like the speeded-up footage of a flower blooming. I hadn't dared to hope I would have this feeling again in my life, and for a few moments I was fearful.

"Is he bothering you?"

I looked round. My neighbor, Senyor Artes, was standing in the entrance to the building. Next to him was the maroon two-wheeled Rolser he always took to the shops with him. Eulogio Faus Artes was in his late sixties, with a drinker's swollen eyelids and gray hair that lay flat against his skull, and he lived on the ground floor, as I did, though his apartment was at the front, facing the street. He was a widower, and rarely had a good word to say about anything. In an attempt to stay on the right side of him, I spoke in Catalan whenever I saw him, Catalan he instantly corrected, even if there was nothing wrong with it, but in the eighteen months that I'd lived in the building he had already taken me to task on several occasions—for putting my rubbish out too early, for letting the door to my apartment slam, and also for playing music in the evenings. Eulogio, I thought. Never had a man been less aptly named.

"He's not bothering me at all," I said. "He's a friend."

"*Friend.*" Artes's lips twisted, then he pushed past me and moved off along the pavement.

"I'm sorry about that," I said, turning back to the young man. "My neighbor isn't very pleasant."

He gave a little shrug. "It's normal."

"It doesn't make you angry?"

"Sometimes." Then, all of a sudden, he looked me full in the face. "But you're not like that."

"I hope not," I said.

He showed me the plastic bag he was holding. "I have come to cook for you."

"You've come to cook for me?"

"Yes. To say thank you."

"How lovely." I took out the keys to my apartment. "Please," I said. "Come in."

HIS NAME was Abdel ben Tajah, he told me, and he was from Tangier. He had been living in Barcelona for about six months. Before that, he was in Almería. He had learned to cook when his mother was knocked down in the street and broke her arm. He was fourteen then. As the eldest of three children, he had to take over in the kitchen. His mother would issue instructions from a nearby chair. No, not like that, he said, imitating her. Cut into smaller pieces. Stir more slowly. You forgot the salt. He was smiling. He hadn't seen her in almost three years. She was still back home, in Morocco.

That evening Abdel cooked a lamb *tajine*. He had arrived with everything that he would need—not just the meat, but tomatoes and onions, dried apricots, fresh coriander, and his own herbs and spices wrapped in twists of rough brown paper. He even brought a terra-cotta cooking pot with a lid. We ate at the small table on my terrace. I lit candles and opened a bottle of Rioja. As a Muslim, Abdel was content with fruit juice. His Spanish was no more sophisticated than my French, and he didn't have any English at all, but we had no trouble communicating. I asked him about Morocco, a country I had never visited. His father's family were Bedouin, he said. They lived in the mountains to the south of Marrakesh. He was open and talkative, nothing like the tense, wary person I had come across in the small hours of Thursday morning. He didn't seem to find it awkward to be alone with a woman from a different culture—a woman he barely knew—and I caught myself hoping it wasn't on account of my age. At least once that evening, while in the bathroom, I leaned close to the mirror, examining my face. People were always telling me how young I looked, how me and my daughter, Mar, could easily be sisters. But that was just something people said, wasn't it. On my way back to the terrace, I paused in the shadows at the far end of the living room. I could see Abdel through the sliding glass door. Gazing out into the night, with his chin propped on one hand, he looked at home, at ease. The fact that I had met him when he was at his lowest had given him, paradoxically, a kind of strength. After all, in his own eyes, he would never be less of a man than he had been on that first night.

It grew late, but the idea that he should leave didn't occur to him. His complacency made me smile, and I had to turn away so he didn't notice. I didn't want him thinking I was mocking him. Busying myself at the sink, I told him I had to be up early in the morning, and that it was probably time he went home. With anyone else, this would have been rude. Not with him, somehow. He stretched lazily, as if he had also drunk a little too much Rioja, then he gathered up his cooking pot, which I had washed, and his remaining herbs and spices, and packed them into the carrier bag he had brought with him. Once I had showed him out of my apartment, we stood on the thin strip of pavement at the front of the building. Aware that my neighbor's living room window was open, I stepped closer to Abdel and spoke in a low voice. I thanked him for cooking for me. He nodded, then studied his feet. For the first time that evening he seemed on edge, as if he was waiting for something, and I remembered how, on Thursday night, I had given him cab fare. He was too embarrassed to bring it up, perhaps.

"Do you need money to get home?" I asked.

"I will take the metro," he said, "or a bus." He turned away, but then turned back. "Did you think about me?"

"I'm sorry?" I wasn't sure I'd understood.

"Did you think about me on Thursday night, after I had gone?" His eyes were earnest and sober, as if the matter troubled him. But I still couldn't work out what he was asking. Before I had time to answer, he spoke again. "I thought about you."

A car came up the narrow street with its headlights on full beam, and as I half-closed my eyes against the glare, one of its wing mirrors clipped my thigh. I let out a faint cry, but the car was already past me and turning onto Avinguda Foix.

Abdel put a hand on my upper arm, near the shoulder. "Are you all right?"

"I'm fine," I said. "It was a shock, that's all."

His hand remained where it was, his gaze intent, unfathomable. He seemed older just then, and I thought I could imagine how he might age, threads of white in those dark curls and fine lines at the edges of his eyes and mouth, but still something extraordinary to look at.

"Really," I said. "It was nothing."

I looked away from him, but felt his gaze rest on me for a moment longer, then he took his hand from my arm and walked off down the street, in the direction of the metro station. I stood and watched him go, his head poised, almost afloat in the air. After what he had said, I could feel my heart beating—it had slowed down, and seemed, at the same time, to have become more powerful, more urgent—and I thought he might look over his shoulder, just a glance, but he didn't, not even once.

A FEW DAYS AFTER Abdel cooked the *tajine*, my ex-husband Pol appeared at my shop. He often dropped in on Saturdays, and he never called beforehand. He knew where I would be, of course—when you run a shop you have to be there all the time, especially if, like me, you can't afford to hire staff—but I always had the feeling there was more to it than that. It was as if he wanted to surprise me, catch me out. As if he was trying to gather evidence for some theory he had about me.

"How much?" He had picked up a Moroccan lantern made of metal and stained glass. Though he knew nothing about Abdel—how could he?—somehow this didn't feel coincidental.

I named a price. "But since it's you," I said, "I could probably go lower."

He smiled, then put it back. "You'll never get rich that way."

Pol owned and ran a management consultancy in Terrassa, an industrial town about half an hour's drive inland, and he lived in a glass-and-concrete house on the west-facing slopes of the Collserola, in an area called La Floresta. After we broke up, he hadn't married again, though he'd had several long-term relationships, usually with women who were much younger. He was as fit as he had been in his twenties—when I was with him, he had been passionate about windsurfing, and he still played tennis three times a week—but as he had aged his face had become leaner, and now that he wore his hair swept back from his forehead and longer at the back, he had a distinctly predatory air. It was as if he had decided to reveal something about himself that had always been true. We had been separated for so long that, had it not been for Mar, it would have been hard for us to believe that we had ever been together, and perhaps for that reason we tended to behave like siblings when we were in each other's company. We joked and bickered and sulked, and in some indefinable way we also still loved each other, though entirely without desire, it seemed, on either part.

I noticed he was wearing jogging bottoms with iridescent stripes down the sides. "Are you seeing someone new?"

He gave me a look that was wary, but also smug.

"Thought so," I said.

"How did you guess?"

I shook my head and looked off into the shop with a remote smile that I knew would annoy him. "I suppose she's—what?—twenty-six?"

Pol laughed. "What about you, Amy? Have you got anyone at the moment?"

"No."

"What happened to the architect?"

"Felip? That ended months ago." I adjusted the position of some notebooks on the counter. "To be honest, it never really began."

"Really? I thought you two were quite well suited."

Pol was being provocative. I had met Felip at a dinner at Montse's house. Felip was divorced and in his early fifties. He talked about buildings the way other people talked about films or books. And he was curious—attentive. We went to bed a couple of times, but it felt slightly awkward, or unequal, as if the act of making love was a pair of scales, and one of us weighed more than the other. He kept giving me things. I wished he would go slower. When I told him I didn't think the relationship was working, about six weeks after the dinner, he said I was acting in haste, and that I hadn't given him a chance. He said I was frightened. It didn't seem to me that any of that was true. Though we no longer saw each other, he would sometimes call me, his voice still hopeful but also forlorn. *How are you? And how is that beautiful shop of yours?*

Pol was checking his phone. "I have to go. Is Mar still arriving on Tuesday?"

I said she was.

"Would it be all right if she stays with me for the first few days, then comes to you on Friday?"

I imagined Pol and his new girlfriend had plans for the weekend, but I wasn't about to hold that against him, or make things difficult.

"No problem," I said.

That evening, I met Montse in a bar in the Barri Gòtic. After Pol's surprise visit, I suppose ex-husbands were on my mind, and as we ordered drinks I remembered that Montse had been married in her twenties, before I knew her, and that her husband, Nacho, had been unfaithful. When I asked her about him, she let out a sigh.

"I made a mistake, love. I was young."

"How long were you together?"

"Getting on for ten years."

At the beginning, she had fallen under his spell completely, she told me. He was a jazz musician, older than her, very cool. He looked at her as if he couldn't quite believe his luck. It was all in his eyes. She felt like the only person in the room. When he played live, he took her with him—to Girona, to Marseille, to Cannes. His drinking didn't bother her back then, maybe because she was drinking too, but later, when she was pregnant with Beatriz, she found she couldn't handle it. He'd come home drunk and start blaming her for things. He never faced up to anything. There was always an excuse. His charm wore thin, like a T-shirt washed too many times. And then there was the cheating...She couldn't go on living with someone like that, children or no children.

The whole time Montse was talking, our waiter had been sending glances in our direction, at both of us, and I was reminded of a phenomenon that I had noticed recently. All of a sudden, around the time of my fortieth birthday, young men began to look at me. Not that they hadn't looked before—they had, when I was young—but this felt like a different kind of gaze. Obviously, I no longer had the body of a seventeen year-old, but neither did I have the neediness I had back then, or the self-regard, and they seemed to pick up on that. It was as if I had grown into a version of myself—or a version of womanhood, perhaps—that they could both desire and appreciate.

I looked at Montse over the rim of my glass. "When you turned forty," I said, "did young men start hitting on you?"

"Are you talking about our waiter?"

I hesitated.

"You are, aren't you." Her penciled eyebrows lifted as she reached for her drink. "Darling, he's just thinking about the expensive trainers you would buy for him."

I stared at her for a moment—this was an angle that would never have occurred to me—then I burst out laughing.

Montse was something else. She really was.

THE FOLLOWING Tuesday I closed early and drove out to the airport. Pol had been planning to pick Mar up, but he'd had a crisis at work, and he had called and asked if I would go instead. Mar was still expecting her father, and when she walked out of Arrivals I thought she looked more grown-up—more of a woman—than she would have done if she'd known I was meeting her.

After we had hugged, she asked where Pol was, but she wasn't put out by the change of plan. The fact that her parents rarely appeared at the same time, and often replaced each other at a moment's notice, was entirely normal. Since she couldn't remember us ever having lived together, our separation hadn't had the slightest effect on her. We talked over each other all the way back to the car. It had been nearly three months.

Once I had negotiated the speed bumps outside the terminal, I accelerated into the left-hand curve that would take us to the city. We passed a giant silver hand holding a mobile phone and a billboard of the Brazilian footballer, Ronaldinho, advertising gum.

"I've always loved the way you drive," Mar said.

"Your father used to give me a hard time about it when you were young. He'd tell me to slow down. Be more responsible."

Mar smiled.

There was a brief silence, then she said, "You look different."

"Oh God," I said. "Have I aged?"

She laughed. "The opposite, if anything. You look weirdly relaxed." Her eyes narrowed. "You're not in love, are you?"

I was careful to conceal my surprise. "I wish."

Despite being in my early twenties when Pol and I split up, I had devoted myself to Mar. I'd had a few relationships—there was the Irish sports journalist, and a sculptor from Valencia—but nothing had lasted. You're still young, Mar told me once, when she was a teenager. You should have a boyfriend. I like things the way they are, I told her. She rolled her eyes. *Mum.* The truth was, I hadn't wanted to disrupt the life I had invented for myself. Infatuations came and went, their white heat hard to sustain. Love was a lower flame, and burned for longer. I knew that. I didn't have the patience for it, though.

I took one hand off the steering wheel and put it against her cheek, not removing it until I had to change gear. "It's so good to have you back. How's England?"

WE STOPPED outside the house in La Floresta, with its facade of smooth gray concrete and its lap pool in the yard. Pol had bought the house in the mid-nineties, not long after he floated his business on the stock market. At that time, property prices had been relatively low. I couldn't imagine what the house must now be worth. His Filipina maid, Ligaya, answered the door, telling Mar her father was on his way, and that he wanted to take her out to dinner. Mar kissed me, then ran upstairs for a shower. I decided not to wait.

I drove back through the Valvidrera tunnels and turned off Via Augusta into Sarrià, calling at my local Caprabo to buy groceries. Half an hour later, when I came round the corner into my street, I saw Abdel standing opposite my building in a white shirt. There was a stirring in me like a glass of water on a café table when a truck goes past. The way the surface of the liquid shudders.

You're not in love, are you?

I pulled up alongside and smiled at him through the open window. 'Have you come to cook for me again?'

He looked uncertain, almost alarmed. "No."

In my nervousness, I had said the first thing that occurred to me. I backtracked quickly. "It was just a joke. Perhaps, this time, I can cook for you."

A car behind me honked, and I told him I needed to find a place to park. I would be back soon.

"Give me the bags," he said. "I will wait here."

"Thank you. That's very kind."

When I returned five minutes later, he carried the shopping into the apartment for me and placed it on the work surface, next to the fridge. I opened the sliding glass door that led to the terrace. The air was thick and still. He started to unpack the bags. I liked the way he didn't speak unless he had something to say. He had no fear of silence, and wasn't embarrassed by it either, even though we hardly knew each other.

I began to put the groceries away. He helped me, passing me the items, one by one. As I reached past him, to place a jar of pickles on a high shelf in the cupboard, my T-shirt lifted clear of my skirt, and he touched me, his fingers brushing the bare skin between my hipbone and my navel. I gasped, as though I'd just been plunged into cold water, then I dropped back onto my heels and turned towards him and we kissed. His hands were under my T-shirt. A car started up below.

We made love on the kitchen floor, the tiles cool beneath me, and then outside, on the terrace. Later, we moved to my bed. At two in the morning, I woke to see his face on the pillow next to mine. He was asleep on his back, one arm flung behind his head. I leaned over and kissed the round bone on the inside of his elbow. Waking, he pulled me on top of him.

The smell of his skin, somehow both sweet and sharp, like honey mixed with paprika. The whiteness of his teeth. I asked him what had happened the previous week. What had he been doing in a car park in Sarrià in the middle of the night? Why had he been so upset?

He turned his face away from me, towards the window, and it was a while before he spoke. "I can't tell you."

"Why not?"

"I'm ashamed."

Once again, I thought of the wet patch on the back of his jeans. This time, though, I felt uneasy.

"There's no need to be ashamed," I said, "not with me."

"Perhaps I will tell you another time."

"You promise?"

"No, I cannot promise."

"All right." I stroked his forehead. "That's all right."

We made love again, but gently now, no urgency about it, and no velocity, as if our real selves were sleeping, and we were simply what was left. Then we too fell asleep, and when I woke up it was beginning to get light. Through the half-open bedroom door I could see part of the kitchen. There was still some shopping to put away.

I SWITCHED ON THE KETTLE and made a pot of tea, using the fresh mint I had bought a day or two before, in the market in Galvany.

"You knew I would come," Abdel said.

I turned. He had been watching me from the bed as I washed the leaves under the cold tap.

"No, I didn't know," I said.

"You knew." He nodded to himself, satisfied that he was right.

My certainty wavered in the face of his. Perhaps, at some level, I *had* known. I must have been thinking of him, at least.

He pulled on his jeans, buttoned his white shirt, and sat down at the table, waiting for me to bring the tea. The stubborn confidence I noticed in him every time I saw him seemed so at odds with his lack of privilege and opportunity. I wondered where it had come from. I couldn't ask him, though. It wouldn't be a question he understood, or knew how to answer. It might even sound like an insult.

I placed the teapot on a tray, along with the cups and the sugar, then I brought it to the table. As I approached, he put his arms round my waist and pressed his face into my belly. My skin began to tingle all over, but I had to hold on to the tray. I couldn't touch him. I had nothing to touch him with.

Later, when I was sitting with my back to the early morning light, I reached for his hand, threading my fingers through his. "After Friday, we can't see each other for two weeks," I said. "My daughter is coming to stay. From England." He looked curious rather than disappointed, as if I had given him the beginning of a story, and he was waiting for the rest. I searched for words to make my meaning clear. "I can't see you, not while she's here."

"Two weeks." He stared at my hand, which still held his.

"It will be hard for me too," I told him.

He looked round at my apartment, and his eyes had the shine and opaqueness of smoked glass.

"No," he said. "It will not be so hard for you."

THAT DAY, when I stepped out of my apartment, Senyor Artes was waiting for me.

"Good morning," I said, careful to address him in Catalan.

"You should be ashamed of yourself." He was spluttering, his voice thick with outrage.

I locked my door, then turned to face him. He was wearing slippers, and leaning on a rustic-looking wooden stick. His cheeks were red, as if he had been slapped.

"I'm sorry?" I said.

He looked at the floor for a moment, and his jaw moved awkwardly from side to side—his teeth were hurting him, perhaps—then he lifted his eyes to me again. "Your apartment is full of cockroaches."

"What?" I blushed, despite myself.

"You let all kinds of vermin into the building. You have no morals. You're filthy—"

"What about your language? Isn't that—"

"You dare to answer back?" He brandished his stick at me. "You're nothing but trash. I'm going to make an example—"

I walked straight past him, trying to close my ears against what he was saying, but his threats and insults followed me. When I was halfway down the street I came to a standstill, shaking. He must have seen Abdel leaving the building that morning—or perhaps he had heard us making love. It was already ten o'clock, and I should have been opening my shop. Instead, I went to Caffe San Marco, on Major de Sarrià. I took a table by the window and ordered a *trifásico,* a coffee with a splash of brandy. The shaking slowly faded. Some people would probably have moved house if they had a neighbor like Senyor Artes, but I refused to consider it. Why should I allow a poisonous old man to ruin my life? Maybe he would work himself up into such a state that he would have some kind of heart attack or stroke. I found myself wishing ill on him. I found myself hoping he would die.

I reached into the back pocket of my jeans and took out a scrap of paper. Earlier, when I told Abdel I couldn't see him for two weeks, he had carefully written down an address and handed it to me.

"So you can find me," he said, "when you are ready."

"This is where you live?"

He nodded.

After he had left, I looked up the address. It was right at the end of the LI line, not far from where the Ronda Litoral turns into the *carretera* that goes all the way to France. Two thoughts struck me as I studied that scrap of paper in San Marco. First, it seemed unlikely that the twenty euros I'd given him on the night we met would have covered a taxi ride to where he lived. Secondly, in order to be waiting casually for me outside my building in one of his neatly ironed shirts, he would have to have traveled for at least an hour on the metro.

WHILE I was in the early stages of my pregnancy, Pol started seeing an ex-girlfriend called Raquel. This was at a time when I believed we were destined for each other, and that we would be together for the rest of our lives. He would meet Raquel at lunchtime, or on his way home from work. They would agree on a place for a rendezvous, then drive there and park their cars. That year, we were renting the ground floor of a modernist house in Valvidrera, a village on the hills at the back of the city. There are plenty of quiet streets in Valvidrera, some of them unpaved and leading off into the wild woodland of the Collserola.

One spring evening, I was sitting on a bench in our small garden when I heard Pol's footsteps on the steeply descending stone steps at the side of the house. The sun had just set behind Montserrat some thirty miles to the west, its famous jagged ridge a forbidding silhouette against all the delicate pink and orange. Pol had called to let me know he would be late, and this time I knew exactly what that meant. I felt desolate, but calm.

"Isn't it a bit cold to be outside?" He stood in front of me with a look of mild concern.

"You're having an affair," I said, "aren't you."

"*What?*"

I held up the packet of condoms I had found in the car at the weekend, wedged between the driver's seat and the door.

"Oh," he said, and almost smiled.

I tossed the packet at his feet and then stood up.

"It doesn't mean anything," he said. "It's not important."

"Have you told her that?"

"Told who?" He stared at me. "What do you mean?"

"Is that what you tell her when you're fucking her? *This doesn't mean anything. This isn't important.*" Anger had bubbled up inside me, bitter as reflux. "I bet that goes down well."

He sighed.

"An affair always means *something*, Pol." I picked up the cup I'd been drinking from and threw it against the side wall of the house. There was a pretty shattering sound, and fragments of blue china appeared as if from nowhere on the gravel near our feet. I heard a window close in the apartment on the second floor.

"Jesus," I said. "How dishonest can you get?"

And then, quite suddenly, all his bravado was gone, and he hung his head and bit his lip, as if he knew he was getting what he deserved. As if it was only fair that I should be allowed to let off steam. As if he just had to weather it, and he'd be off the hook. His patronizing attitude lit a fuse in me, and I exploded.

"You know what?" I said. "This is over."

"This what?"

"This stupid marriage."

"What?" he said. "Just like that?"

"Just like that."

"But we're having a baby—"

"*I'm* having a baby. You're off fucking other people in our car."

A cunning look stole onto Pol's face. He was like that. He could change in an instant, and smoothly, like the ads on bus shelters. One moment, it's eye shadow. The next, it's a betting shop. Or pizza. His voice became soft, insinuating. "This is all a bit convenient, isn't it."

Now I was the one who didn't understand.

"You actually *wanted* me to screw up," he went on, his voice still held down, but growing in assurance. "You've been looking for an excuse."

Though I resented the way he had turned the tables on me, as if I was the one in the wrong, I considered what he'd just said. "You know, I think you might be onto something there."

He stared at me in disbelief, then bent down and began to gather up the pieces of blue china.

"You broke my favorite cup," he muttered.

Our marriage dragged on for several months, but it was over not long after Mar was born. The separation was amicable, in that there were no fierce arguments over custody and maintenance—my willingness to stay on in Barcelona made things easier—though not so amicable that our friends didn't have to choose sides, at the beginning at least. So why did I get rid of him? I allowed people to think it was all about betrayal, and they believed it, especially the women, because Catalan women are fiery and proud, and will not tolerate humiliation—as Montse told me once, years later, *When Nacho cheated on me, I wanted to tear his heart out and throw it on the ground and stamp on it*—but I saw Pol's infidelity as a symptom of something else, something I found harder to forgive. There was a weakness in him. A craven quality. The way his gloating dissolved into self-pity. *You broke my favorite cup.* I wanted a man who would stand up for me, and for himself. Was that too much to ask?

I kept remembering how he had accused me of having waited for an excuse to end the relationship, and the look of thinly disguised triumph as he realized he had stumbled on a kind of truth. He had surprised me, but he had also surprised himself. I remembered how he had rounded on me, believing he had gained the upper hand, and how he seemed to crumple when I said he might be onto something. He had imagined I would start denying it, or I would lose my temper, or simply give in, terrified at the thought of losing him... The one thing he hadn't bargained for was that I would agree with him, and I wasn't sure he had ever forgiven me for that.

IT WAS ANOTHER HOT, airless night, and Mar had gone out. She was seeing friends in Castelldefels, and I had let her borrow my car. When she told me she'd probably be late, I suggested she stay over and bring the car back in the morning. I didn't want her driving drunk—I'd always been strict about such things—but at the same time I sensed an ulterior motive on my part. Sometimes your body understands before you do. I showered and changed into a clean T-shirt and a pair of jeans, then I walked to the metro and caught a train that was going downtown. When I got off at Plaça Catalunya, I almost lost my nerve. Suppose I took an escalator up to Las Ramblas, as though that had been my intention all along? I could wander the streets of the Barri Gòtic. Drop in on my friend

Neus, who lived near Santa María del Mar. But then I thought of Abdel, and something inside me tightened. I stood in the circular concourse, with people milling all around me. I had told him we wouldn't be able to see each other for two weeks, and he had done as I had asked and kept away. What if it had been too easy for him? What if he had forgotten about me? I was happy to have my daughter back—of course I was—but there had been something barren or hollow about the last few days, as though I'd been on a sort of hunger strike. I had to see him, if only for a minute...

Turning my back on the escalator that led up to the street, I followed the signs to the red line, direction Fondo. On the platform, the air was heavily spiced. Mingled smells of burnt coffee grounds and sweat. Fried garlic too. I stood by the wall, one knee bent, the sole of my shoe flat against the tiles. *Fondo.* In some ways, it was an obvious name for the last station on the line, since one meaning of *fondo* was "end." But it could also mean "stamina," and it could mean "essence" too, or "heart," in the figurative sense, as in "the heart of the city." There was nothing about the word that didn't feel relevant. A train slammed out of the dark tunnel, pushing my hair across my face. The silver doors slid open. I stepped into a carriage and found a seat. The middle-aged South American woman sitting opposite smiled at me. It was as if she knew what I was up to, and approved. I smiled back. Though the train was air-conditioned, the gleam on the woman's skin told me how hot it was outside. I lifted my eyes to the map of the LI line. Thirteen stops to go.

I thought of my daughter driving down the coast road to Castelldefels, past the Repsol petrol station with its dusty, sunlit forecourt, past the cement factory at El Garraf, a Heath Robinson–like arrangement of pipes and chimneys, past shady nightclubs like the Saratoga and the Riviera. I took out my phone. Seeing I had a signal, I called her number.

"Mum?" she said. "Are you all right?"

I felt a sudden rush of love for her. It was physical, like a lump in my throat, and I had to speak past it. "You'll stay over if you drink, won't you."

Mar laughed. "That's about the fifteenth time you've said that."

"You promise?"

"I promise. Where are you, anyway? I can hardly hear you."

"I'm on the metro."

"You didn't say you were going out. I wouldn't have taken the car if I'd known."

"I didn't know I was going out until after you left—and anyway, I like the metro."

She was laughing again. "You're crazy. I've got a crazy mother."

But it was true, actually. I did like the metro. All those names, so exotic and unpronounceable—to start with, at least: Urquinaona, El Putxet, Llacuna, Gorg. And the way the faces changed, according to which line you traveled on. Even after twenty years in the city, I often felt like a tourist.

When I got off at Fondo, it was clear that I had reached the end of the line. The paved area outside the station was littered and desolate, and the facades of the buildings crawled with graffiti. For a moment, I felt like turning round and taking a train straight back to Plaça Catalunya—

Wait, I told myself. You're here now. You don't have to do anything. Just find out where he lives, then go...

But my insides twisted at the thought of seeing him.

While at home, I had studied a map of the city. It was a ten-minute walk from the metro to the address he had given me. I'd decided not to bring the map, though. Instead, I'd learned the route by heart. I wouldn't feel comfortable if I appeared not to know my way around. I set off up the main road. An apartment block loomed overhead, most of its windows open. People were washing up, arguing. TVs were on full blast. Sound systems too. There was a bar on the corner, its door ajar. An old man in a white vest gestured to the woman leaning on the counter, his movements so slow he might have been underwater. It seemed hotter out here, on the city's edge. To cool myself down, I lifted my hair away from my neck, then let it drop.

In no time, I left the apartment blocks behind and found myself in an area that was even more neglected. The curbstones broken, potholes everywhere. I took a right turn into a narrow street that ran uphill. Brick buildings stood on one side. They looked as if they might be used as garages or storage units. On the other side was a row of shops, their metal grilles drawn down for the night and padlocked at ground level. Up ahead, in the fall of light from a streetlamp, I saw a long table set up on the pavement. The plastic chairs were all different colors. Sun-faded pink, ocean blue. Mint green. I moved closer, then stopped. Half a dozen North African men were sitting about in T-shirts and flip-flops, some playing cards, others smoking hookahs. The air smelled of sweet apple. Among them was Abdel, his leg dangling over the arm of a chair, one hand against the back of his head. My heart seemed to leap inside me and then dive deep, leaving ripples to spread through me, and in that moment a tall man in a djellaba said something, and all their faces turned in my direction, curious, but not inhospitable.

Abdel rose from his chair and walked over to where I was standing. One hand on my back, he guided me into the light and addressed the people gathered there.

"This is Amy," he said. "She's a good friend." His French was simple, as if it was me he was talking to. As if he wanted to make sure I understood. "She helped me when I needed help. She was kind to me."

There were murmurs of welcome, and people made room for me. A plate of dates and nuts was placed in front of me. Fruit juice was poured into a paper cup.

After fifteen minutes, Abdel spoke into my ear. "We can leave now."

He led me away from the table and off along the street.

"Is that your family?" I asked.

He nodded. "An uncle and some cousins."

The moment we turned the corner, he reached for me and pulled me close. His mouth tasted of the pear juice he had been drinking.

"In here," he said.

I followed him through a gap in the wall, over a pile of rubble, and on into a building that was still under construction. We climbed bare concrete stairs. The air felt cooler. On the top floor we came out into a spacious room. There was no glass in the windows, and I leaned on the sill, looking out over the low rooftops to the east. A strip of black sea showed. There were pinpricks of light where a ship lay anchored.

He was standing behind me, close to me, his breath against my neck. I turned to face him. After kissing me, he knelt on the floor, undid my jeans, and slowly pulled them down. I pushed both my hands into his hair. He kissed the inside of my thighs. My breathing thickened, and I was trembling. The muscles in my legs lost all their strength. I don't think I could have walked. When he stood up, I unzipped his trousers and slid one hand inside. He maneuvered me away from him. Folded me over the sill. I felt the part of me that might have questioned what I was doing fly off into the night, fast as a flung stone. That part of me would know nothing. Forget it was ever there. The rest of me shook as if with cold.

I glanced over my shoulder. "Do you have something?"

His hand opened. The glint of silver foil.

"Let me do it," I said.

I tore the packet open, then dropped to my knees in front of him, taking him in my mouth before unrolling the condom. He drew the air in past his teeth, his stomach hollowing. I stood up again and bent over the sill. A mound of gravel three floors down, dim light on a puddle. He leaned past my shoulder. Found my mouth with his. My head twisted to the right, I felt him enter me. Still behind me, he reached for my breasts. I closed my eyes, then gasped as he pushed deeper.

His breathing speeded up. I had to bite my forearm to keep from crying out.

Later, when he had finished, I opened my eyes and saw that I was high above the ground. TV aerials on rooftops, the dark ribbon of the sea. A cargo boat at anchor. I had forgotten where I was, and even though my eyes were open the view still seemed unreal. What was I doing in this place?

We stood at an angle to each other, straightening our clothes. His eyes were lowered, his expression serious.

"One day, this will be a bedroom," I said. "People will make love here." I looked around, trying to imagine it. A carpet, curtains. Wallpaper. "We were the first, though."

I smiled at him, and he smiled back, but I had the feeling he wasn't sure what I was saying. I glanced at my watch. Half past eleven. If I left now, I could catch the metro.

"I have to go," I said.

He led me back down the stairs. My legs still felt unsteady. I wondered who would buy the place. Would they ever guess what had happened in their home while it was being built?

Out on the street we kissed again. It was hard to stop.

At last, I broke away and looked back up the road. He seemed to understand that I might find it embarrassing to walk past his family. He told me of another route to the station. It was quicker, he said. "Shall I walk with you?"

I shook my head. "There's no need. Really."

We said goodbye.

There was a shift in the air, and I thought I could smell the seashore. Fish heads, engine oil. Rust. I was tired suddenly, and longed to be back in my apartment.

I had been aware of traffic in the distance—the Ronda Litoral wasn't far away—but now there was another noise, closer and more urgent. The vicious insect buzzing of a two-stroke motorbike. When I looked round, I saw nothing except a blinding headlight, the figure of a rider behind it, shadowy and indistinct. My shoulder jerked, as if I had been hit by a solid, padded weight. The force of it knocked me off my feet. Only when I sat up in the gutter did I realize my bag was gone.

"Fuck," I muttered.

The bike's engine had died away, and I was alone. The night was warm and brackish, as before. Apartment buildings showed fewer lights. My shoulder stung and throbbed, but I didn't think anything was broken.

I climbed shakily to my feet, then pulled my T-shirt away from my body and looked inside. A graze curved past my right breast and under my armpit where the strap had resisted for a second before it snapped. The whole thing had happened so fast. All I could remember was the rapidly expanding glare of the headlight and the snarl of the engine, and then the blow to my shoulder. I couldn't have described the make of the motorbike. I couldn't even have described the color. I had no memory of a license plate. How many assailants had there been? One—or two? I couldn't have said. And now that I glanced round I saw that I was only a couple of steps from safety—for there, lit with a faint white glow, was the escalator that led down into Fondo metro station.

I checked the pockets of my jeans. Luckily, I still had my phone. But I had nothing else. No credit cards, no keys. Still, the phone was something.

I called Mar and told her I'd been mugged.

Alarm rushed into her voice. "Are you all right?"

I said I was. I had no money, though, and no way of getting home. I asked if she could come and pick me up. There was a silence on the other end.

"I'm sorry to ruin your evening."

"No, no, it's fine," she said. "I was thinking of leaving anyway."

"Are you all right to drive?"

"I only had one beer. Where are you?"

"Fondo."

"*Where?*"

"I'm outside the Fondo metro station. It's in the northeast of the city. Sant Andreu."

Another silence.

"That's going to take me a while," she said.

"Don't worry," I said. "I'll wait."

I sat on a bench near the main entrance. I could always have walked back to where Abdel lived—I was sure he would have helped—but it was too late for that now. I had asked Mar to come. The Rambla del Fondo stretched away into the distance, its central reservation planted with trees. There was also a red *M* on a pole, signaling a second entrance. The sky above me was smothered with clouds. It looked marbled, like the endpaper from some nineteenth-century book.

I had been waiting for about an hour when a car pulled up nearby. Behind the wheel was a man in his forties, his tie loosened, his shirtsleeves rolled. The window on the driver's side slid down. He asked me if I needed a lift somewhere.

"My daughter's picking me up," I said. "She should be here any minute. But thank you."

"Well, all right. If you're sure..." He continued to look at me, concern in his eyes, then he shifted into gear and drove away.

Not long afterwards, I saw my own car approaching, Mar's face in the windscreen.

Once inside, I put my arms round her. "Thanks so much for coming." She had the air-conditioning on, and her skin and hair felt cool.

Sitting back, I saw she had a strange, stubborn look I recognized from when she was younger. It would appear when I did something she didn't associate with me. When I seemed to be acting out of character. It was as if she was determined to hold on to some idea she had of me and ignore all evidence to the contrary, even if it was happening right in front of her eyes. Her gaze shifted from my face to what lay beyond me—the utilitarian apartment blocks, the graffiti, the streetlamps' brownish-yellow light.

"You really have a friend out here?" She sounded, in that moment, exactly like her father.

"I have all kinds of friends," I said. "Some aren't as well-off as others."

She appeared to think about this. Politically, of course, she couldn't disapprove. Still, it had come as a surprise to her. It's only natural, perhaps, for children to believe their parents lead narrow lives. It originates in the idea they have of you, that you're someone who can be predicted, counted on—someone safe. Perhaps it's even a necessary belief, since it allows them to rebel against you. Be dangerous themselves.

"So they took your bag?" she said.

"Yes."

"You're not hurt, though."

"No. I was lucky, wasn't I?" I put my hand on her shoulder, then stroked her hair. "I'm sorry if you were worried. I didn't mean to worry you."

"You should be more careful."

She glanced in her rearview mirror, then pulled away from the curb. She didn't seem to mind that her evening had been interrupted. If she was upset or angry, it was because I'd got into trouble. Your mother wasn't supposed to be somebody who needed help. Your mother was the one who came to the rescue. Everything was the wrong way round.

It was only later, as we passed through the tunnel beneath Plaça d'Alfonso Comín, that I wondered if she had smelled Abdel on me when I got into the car and gave her a hug. Though I hadn't lied exactly, maybe she had seen through my talk of "a friend." Was that the real reason why her face had taken on that stubborn look?

I WOKE AT SEVEN-THIRTY, after only three or four hours' sleep, and went into the kitchen. Not wanting to disturb Mar, I left the radio off and moved quietly, on bare feet. I drank my coffee on the terrace, then watered the geraniums.

The sun was already coloring the tops of nearby buildings. The yellow awning on a penthouse terrace glowed. To the south and high up there was a long, thin cloud that was semi-transparent. It looked as if a huge hand had idly dragged a piece of white chalk across the blue.

Later, as I pulled on some clothes, I noticed that the self-inflicted bite mark on my arm had almost faded. I remembered the view from that unfinished house—the jumbled rooftops and aerials, the anchored boat—and an echo of that snatched pleasure went through me like a shudder. I took Mar's keys, leaving her a note, then let myself out of the apartment.

The far end of my street was an inch deep in pale gray dust, like the surface of the moon. Some bags of cement must have fallen off the back of a truck during the night. I crossed Avinguda Foix and climbed a slope that led past the dog park. Hector was standing on the beige dirt in a red T-shirt, with his arms folded, while Rocky cocked his leg against a tree. I waved at him, and he waved back, his glasses flashing in the morning light.

The local police station stood among palm trees and shrubbery on the top of a small hill. With its fawn-colored stucco facade and its ornamental battlements, the building looked like a castle in a fairy tale, and when Mar was young the two of us would make up stories about it. The chief of the Guardia Urbana was a man called Grau. He had gaps between his teeth and a foul temper—he was always shouting and slamming doors—so we cast him in the role of ogre. Mar shocked me by suggesting that he ate the people he arrested.

The undergrowth that surrounded the police station was home to a number of stray cats. The old woman who came twice a day to feed them was almost as feral as they were. We would often see her, hunched over, muttering. She was obviously a witch, Mar told me. If so, I said, perhaps she had cast a spell over the chief of police. He might appear to be an ogre, but it would only take one kiss to turn him back into a handsome prince. Well, *I'm* not kissing him, was Mar's response.

That morning, I was interviewed by a broad-shouldered officer with a shaved head. I knew I had no chance of seeing my bag again, I told him, but I thought I should report the incident all the same. He listened without interrupting, making occasional notes on the pad that lay in front of him. When I mentioned Sant Andreu, his head lifted. I continued with my account—how late it was, the empty road, a motorbike that came from nowhere...

"Lucky the strap broke," he said, "otherwise you might have been dragged." He looked at me steadily. "Were you hurt?"

"Not really. Just a graze."

I began to list the contents of my bag, then I stopped. I had just realized that I had lost the thin gold ring Pol had bought for me while we were traveling in Crete. This was in the mid-eighties, when we were still in love, my daughter not yet gathering inside me. I remembered the gleam of the gold, so soft and yellow. Almost buttery. Its coolness as it slid onto my finger. I remembered the gray marble floor in the jewelry shop, and how I held my hand out in the air, my fingers spread, and I thought of all the years that had slipped through them, more than twenty. So much was over and done with, and soon to be forgotten altogether. I felt there was less of me than there had been before, as if time itself had diminished me. I was crying.

The policeman passed me a couple of tissues. I thanked him, then told him about the ring.

"We're not together any more," I said. "We haven't been together for a long time. Somehow that makes it worse—the loss of something that's already gone…" I shook my head. "I'm sorry. I shouldn't be bothering you with all this."

His eyes circled the room. "It's not exactly busy round here."

I wasn't sure this was true, but it was his way of saying that he wouldn't hurry me, and I was grateful for his tact, his grace.

"You don't have to answer this," he said, "but I feel I have to ask. What took you to Sant Andreu?"

"I was visiting a friend."

"That surprises me."

"Really? Why?"

He shrugged. "A woman like you…"

I watched him, but didn't speak.

"Put it this way," he said. "It's a long way from Sarrià."

I thought of Abdel, and wanted him inside me again.

I cleared my throat. "I should have been more careful," I said. "I was feeling happy. I wasn't paying attention."

The policeman seemed to realize I was hiding something, but he chose not to pursue it.

"What do you do for a living?" he asked.

"I have a shop." I described it for him.

"I know the place." He put down his pen and leaned back in his chair. His face relaxed. "It's my mother's birthday next month. Maybe I'll drop in and buy something for her."

"Please do." Smiling, I stood up. "And thank you for being so understanding."

A BUILDING SITE?" Montse lit a cigarette and blew the smoke out of one side of her mouth, as if it was interfering with her thought process. "Are you out of your mind?"

"Not so loud," I said. "It's a secret, remember?"

"What's a secret?"

Montse's husband, Jaume, had appeared in the kitchen doorway.

I was at their house for dinner. As sometimes happened, they had tried to set me up with somebody they knew. Josep—or Pep, as he was known—was the finance director of a prestigious perfume company. He had lost his Japanese wife in a car accident five years before, Montse had told me on the phone, but he was "over it," apparently. Also, she had added wickedly, he was loaded. We hadn't hit it off, though, and he'd left early.

"You wouldn't be interested," Montse told Jaume.

"Is it Amy's secret?" he asked.

We looked at him, but said nothing.

Jaume smiled. "How could I possibly *not* be interested?" But he didn't linger. Fetching a bottle of cognac, he moved back onto the terrace, where the other guests sat talking in the candlelight.

Once he had gone, I turned to Montse again.

"It's crazy, I know," I said. "There are times when life just seems completely unbelievable."

"I can't remember the last time I felt like that."

"That's the point. It's part of being young, I think, that unbelievability. It's not that you expect it. It's just that it keeps happening. It's because you don't know any different, and because there are no limits. Later on, things start taking on a shape. The possibilities seem—I don't know—*fewer* somehow, or even nonexistent—" I stopped myself. "I'm rambling. I must be drunk."

Montse shrugged, then lit another cigarette.

There was a brief silence.

"Poor Pep," she said. "He didn't stand a chance."

Suddenly, we were in hysterics. That was how it was with Montse—everything tipping, sooner or later, into hilarity, as if the whole of life was on a slide, with laughter at the bottom.

We went to join the others on the terrace, where Jaume was talking with great urgency about the wave that was coming. Wave? Montse said. What wave? A financial crash, Jaume said. It was already happening in the United States. Europe would be next. All our lives were going to change. People thought he was exaggerating, or being pessimistic, and the conversation turned to the subject of the drought. It hadn't rained for months, and the levels in reservoirs in Catalunya had dropped by 75 percent. There were rumors that water would be brought in by tanker from places like Tarragona and Marseille. As I sat down, Jaume glanced my way and raised both eyebrows, as if I had done something to impress him, and I wondered if he'd been in the kitchen doorway for longer than we realized and heard more than he was supposed to.

That night, I was the last to leave. When I got up from the table, Jaume offered to call me a taxi. I told him I'd prefer to walk. It was downhill all the way, I said. It would only take me twenty minutes.

"You're sure?" he said. "After what just happened?"

"I'm not likely to get mugged twice in a week—and anyway, this is Sarrià."

Jaume smiled. "All right. But call us when you get home."

"This is like being seventeen again," I said to Montse.

She gave me a look. "In more ways than one."

I set off down Avinguda Valvidrera, the moon at the top of the sky and seemingly caught in a net of cloud. Saturday night. My head spinning from all the wine. Stopping on the bridge over the Ronda, I leaned on the rail, the six-lane highway fifty feet below. Traffic rushed beneath me, north to the Costa Brava, or south to Castelldefels and Sitges. Exhaust fumes mingled with frangipani...

Moving on, I rounded the roundabout, then turned into Major de Sarrià. The narrow street curved downhill between tall thin houses. Everything was shut. I crossed Bonanova, then walked through the square where the church was and on past Casa Rafael, a little place where I sometimes went for lunch. A light wind circled me.

And then it happened.

A man lurched out of a side street ahead of me, gray flannel trousers flapping round legs that were impossibly long.

He must have been seven and a half feet tall. He wore a dark shirt that was untucked, and his hair, which was also dark, had been cut in an old-fashioned style, with a side parting. He passed in front of me with lengthy, cantilevered strides, as if his feet were only loosely bolted to his ankles. Perhaps he sensed my presence, though, because he stopped in the middle of Major de Sarrià and turned to face me, and when he spoke his voice was light, almost a tenor, not the deep, hoarse bass I would have expected.

"Are you lost?"

I laughed. "Do I look lost?"

He seemed to take the question seriously, but chose not to answer. Instead, he put a finger inside the collar of his shirt, as if it was chafing him.

"I'm on my way home," I said. "I live close by." I indicated the street beyond him, but he continued to look at me. "I'm sorry," I went on. "I didn't mean to stare. It's just that you startled me, appearing suddenly like that. I suppose I thought I was alone." I paused. "Also, to be honest, I've had a bit too much to drink."

"I thought I was alone as well."

He smiled, and I smiled too. His face was all dents and hollows, suggesting the huge skull that lay beneath.

"Would you like me to escort you?" he asked.

"Oh no," I said. "No, thank you. I'm nearly there."

"Well, good night."

"Good night."

He lifted one hand in a gesture of farewell and then moved on into Carrer de Monterols.

As I watched him go, his head almost on a level with the first-floor balconies, I thought of the procession that took place in Sarrià every September, during the *Festa Major,* something children always looked forward to. Papier-mâché giants—or *gigants,* as they were known—were built in the image of monarchs or aristocrats or even local celebrities. Ten feet tall, maybe more, they were paraded through the streets, with people inside them, both to carry them and to maneuver them. When they passed by, they would slowly and solemnly turn this way and that, as if to acknowledge the crowds that had gathered. The giants were an expression of local identity and culture, and their presence on that one day of the year represented a kind of blessing. In that moment I felt I had also just been blessed, and as I approached my apartment I took out my phone and called Montse.

"Are you home?" Montse asked. "We were getting worried—"

Looking back along the street, I talked over her. "Something extraordinary just happened."

THE NEXT DAY was Sunday, my day off, and I slept late, waking at ten to find I was alone in the apartment. As I stepped out of the shower, the front door opened and Mar appeared. She had bought croissants, freshly squeezed orange juice, and the newspapers in English and *castellano.* She had discovered a new bakery, she said, near Plaça Artos. I gave her a kiss and told her she was the best daughter ever. Later, I called one of my favorite restaurants—*Agua*—and booked a table for lunch. Mar would be going back to Bristol in a day or two, and I wanted to take her somewhere special.

That afternoon, we drove down to Barceloneta. The coolness of Via Laietana, which always seemed to be in the shade, no matter what time of day it was. Then the port, the masts of boats swaying and clicking in the offshore breeze, the sunlight glassy, dazzling. We found a place to park, and by a quarter to three we were sitting at a simple wooden table that overlooked the beach. We ordered fresh asparagus and pasta with crayfish, and drank cold white wine and Vichy Catalan.

Halfway through the meal, Mar's face swung towards me suddenly, as if she'd been fighting an urge until that moment, but could fight no longer.

"What's going on, Mum?"

I knew I couldn't duck the question, or pretend not to understand. I had felt it coming for some time. Ever since the night my bag was snatched, I had sensed a fidgety quality in her. When we were in the same room, she would glance at me if she thought I wasn't looking, and when we ate together one of her knees would be jiggling under the table.

"I wasn't going to tell you," I said. "I didn't think you needed to know."

"Shouldn't I be the judge of that?"

"You might not like it."

She shrugged.

"All right," I said. "If you're sure."

I started at the beginning, with the sound of somebody crying in the middle of the night, and then I just kept going, and though the story felt natural, the way one moment fed into the next, I could see that it easily outstripped whatever Mar might have had in mind. She had stopped eating, and had slumped lower in her chair, her eyes unreadable behind her sunglasses, a tension in her mouth and jaw.

"Don't worry," I said. "There's no way it can last." I looked out to sea, where a dinghy with a light-green sail slid across the blue. "Right now, though, it's as strong as anything I've ever known." I reached for my wine and drank.

"Jesus."

I glanced at her, but she was looking past me, along the promenade.

"I shouldn't have told you," I said.

"Do you love him?"

"It's not love. At least, I don't think it is."

"What is it, then?"

I put down my glass. "Didn't you always say I should have a boyfriend?"

For a few moments Mar didn't react, but then she met my gaze and we both began to laugh. People at neighboring tables glanced in our direction, and when we saw their puzzled smiles we laughed even harder, partly because we knew things they didn't know, and partly because we were just as puzzled as they were.

ONCE MAR HAD FLOWN back to the UK, Abdel started visiting again. I would turn the corner, into my street, and there he would be, leaning against the brick wall next to the photocopying shop. I didn't mention the fact that I'd been robbed. It would only make him feel guilty for not having walked me to the metro, and I didn't want him feeling any guilt. He appeared every three or four days, through the rest of August and on into September. There were evenings when we went to Bar Tomás—he loved Quique, the head waiter, with his leg that dragged and his growling voice, his kindness hidden underneath, like an embarrassing condition—or if it was too hot to be indoors we would have a drink in the square by the church. I couldn't help noticing how the difference in our ages was obscured by the way in which he took control of certain situations. It was a version of maleness that seemed to come naturally to him, and must have had its roots in his culture. He made me feel younger just by being himself. Sometimes I felt younger than he was.

On a warm evening in the first week of October, I took him to a restaurant in Sarrià for the first time. We sat in a walled garden, under a palm tree, and he told me about his new job at a factory that manufactured laminated glass. He was proud to have been hired, but the work was hard and the hours were long. He showed me his hands. There were cuts on the inside of his fingers, and the base of his thumb had an inch-long gash in it. His palms had become as rough as sandpaper. I saw no trace of resentment or self-pity on his face, but sometimes he looked at me as if he was hoping I might change his life for him. I couldn't do that, though—could I? When he turned twenty-six, I would be fifty.

We didn't talk much that evening. We just ordered, and ate, and smiled at each other, the night air curling round us. It seemed enough to sit in silence, imagining the love that would happen later, in my apartment. I remember only one exchange, and it was the one I'd thought he would prohibit.

"I have to ask you about that night," I said.

"Again?" He looked away from me, into the garden.

"I need to know what happened." I put my hand on his hand. "It's how everything began."

He was avoiding my eyes, and his face was somber, almost desolate, like someone who is about to be evicted and has nowhere to go.

"Tell me," I said.

He took a breath and let it out slowly. "I sold myself," he said in a low voice, looking at the table. "To men."

The moment he opened his mouth, I somehow knew what he was going to say. Perhaps I had known all along.

"Did you use condoms?"

His head came up, and he stared at me, wide-eyed. "Is that all you can say?"

"It's important—and not just for you. For me too."

He looked away from me again. "I had no life to lose. That's what I thought."

I brought his scarred hand to my lips and held it there, no longer conscious of where I was, not seeing anything at all.

"Yes," I heard him say, as if across a great distance. "I always used condoms." He seemed to hesitate. "Except once. The night we met."

That night, he went on, the man who had picked him up forced him to do things he didn't want to do. The man was English. He drove an expensive car. A Lexus. It was black.

I began to cry.

He put his other hand against my face.

"When I saw you in the car park," he went on, "I thought you might be his wife."

"His wife?"

"I don't know why."

Abdel paid the bill, even though he had no money. He insisted on it. Then we walked back to my apartment.

We crossed Bonanova, then took a right turn, past the church. Up against the side wall was a hidden *plaçeta*—a small square—with tall trees and a couple of benches. During the day you would see skateboarding teenagers or Roma people with paper begging cups. At night it was usually deserted. We stopped beneath a first-floor apartment, its French windows open, no curtains. I heard a burst of static. Someone was trying to tune a radio. The ceiling of the room was white with dark wooden beams. Another crackle, then piano music, clear as water. I leaned against Abdel in the shadows under the wrought-iron balcony. His white shirt, my sleeveless dress. Almost nothing separating my skin from his...

Later, when we rounded the corner into my street, my heart turned over. Senyor Artes was standing in front of my apartment building, smoking a cigar and leaning on his cane. He looked like someone sampling the air before setting off into the night, but that, I knew, was as far as he would go. To enter the lobby, we would have to pass right by him. I thought about doubling back and walking round the block. Waiting until he went inside. At that same moment, Abdel noticed Senyor Artes, and I felt him slow down, his hand pulling on mine.

"Perhaps it's better if I go," he said.

"No," I said. "This is my home." I faced him, smiling. "I don't want you to go."

He nodded, though he still looked troubled.

I took out my keys, hoping we might slip past the old man, but he had positioned himself so as to bar the entrance, like some self-appointed guardian of the building.

"Excuse me, Senyor," I said.

Artes didn't even glance at me. Instead, he fixed Abdel with a look of contempt and drew on his cigar.

I put a hand on the old man's arm. "Please let us in."

He shook me off. "Not him."

"*What?*" I laughed in disbelief.

Artes continued to stare at Abdel, then he turned and spat on the pavement, just to one side of the entrance. I took advantage of the momentary lapse in his attention to try and push my way into the lobby, but he lashed out with his stick, catching Abdel across the face. I gave the old man a shove. The pavement was narrow, only three or four feet wide, and as he staggered backwards he was struck by a passing car. It was only a glancing blow, but he fell awkwardly. The car braked and stopped. Its headlights showed me the street as it stretched away towards Avinguda Foix. Abdel was standing up against the outside wall of the building. There was a bruise on his cheek. Some blood too.

The car door opened. The man who got out was wearing a blue-and-white-striped shirt and a pair of chinos. He looked at Senyor Artes, who was lying half on the pavement and half in the road, then his eyes lifted to mine. "You pushed him."

"He fell," I said.

"You pushed him in front of my car. I saw you." He crouched next to Artes. The old man's eyes were closed, and his face had stiffened. His stick lay in the gutter.

Another car approached. When the second driver—a woman—saw the road was blocked, she honked twice.

I turned to Abdel, who was still standing by the wall. "You should leave."

He didn't seem to understand.

"Please go," I said.

The driver of the first car glanced over his shoulder, putting out a hand. "No one's leaving."

"Go," I said to Abdel. "Now."

Abdel moved uncertainly along the pavement in the direction of Avinguda Foix, his back lit by the headlights.

I bent down next to the driver. "Is he badly hurt?"

"I don't know. I think he hit his head." He punched a few buttons on his phone. "I'm calling an ambulance."

"Of course," I said. "That's right."

I was shivering, though the night was just as warm as before.

The woman in the second car was standing behind her open door. "What happened?"

"He hit my friend," I told her. "He hit him in the face."

I sat down on the curb, my forearms resting on my knees, my mind buzzing, blank. At least Abdel had got away. That was all I cared about. A phrase my father used to use floated into my head. *It'll end in tears.* But this was a story that had begun in tears.

In the distance I heard a siren.

SENYOR ARTES DIED in the ambulance, on the way to hospital. The next day I was summoned to the police station on the hill, where I was questioned by Grau, the bad-tempered chief who had once featured in my fairy tales. Having taken depositions from other witnesses—including, presumably, the driver of the car—Grau didn't think the death of Senyor Artes could be dismissed as a simple traffic accident, and he arranged for my immediate transfer to the local headquarters of the Mossos d'Esquadra, the division of the police that dealt with violent crimes like rape and murder. Since there was no such thing as manslaughter in Spain, he told me, I would be charged with something called "imprudent homicide." I was in a daze. I'd had no sleep, and everything seemed to be happening behind a sheet of glass.

During my first interview in the station on Iradier Street, I admitted to having had a relationship with Abdel ben Tajah, the man who had "fled the scene," as they put it, though I claimed not to know where he was living. The police officer running the investigation—a man by the name of Bernardo Lull—didn't believe me. He produced an official report, stating that my bag had recently been snatched in Sant Andreu. Which coincidentally, he added, watching me closely, was an area known to be populated by Moroccans. As you say, I murmured. Coincidentally. Lull was still watching me. Abdel would always come to Sarrià, I explained. We would see each other in my apartment. That, after all, was how we'd met. But Senyor Artes had disapproved of me seeing—or even knowing—a Moroccan. Artes had been a racist of the worst kind. Lull kept returning to the same question. If I had no address or phone number for the Moroccan—he called Abdel "the Moroccan"—how would I contact him? I didn't contact him, I said. He would just appear. Whenever he felt like it? Grau interjected, with a sneer. I nodded. For me, I said, it was never often enough. Lull changed his approach. Was he employed? He had a job in a glass factory, I said, but he didn't like to talk about it. I think he was ashamed of it. Once again, Grau stepped in. If he was *ashamed,* it was probably because he was a rent boy. It was probably because he *sold* himself. Obviously, they'd been saving this piece of information for the moment when they thought it would unnerve or provoke me the most. As before, I remained quite calm. I knew about that, I said. He told me. Lull and Grau exchanged a glance, then left the room.

Abdel hadn't done anything wrong, I told Lull later that day, when he returned, alone. Senyor Artes had hit Abdel in the face with his walking stick, but he had chosen not to retaliate. If Artes had lived, I added, Abdel would have had every right to bring charges against him. For assault. So why did he run? Lull asked. He didn't *want* to run, I said. I told him to. Lull asked why I would do something like that. Because I didn't want him to become involved, I said. Because I wanted to protect him. Lull found that strange. Surely he would have been useful as a witness, he said. Invaluable, in fact. I shook my head. He was an illegal immigrant, I said. As if that wasn't bad enough, he had also spent time working in the sex trade, as Lull's colleague in the Guardia Urbana had been so eager to point out. Did he—Lull—really believe that a jury would listen to someone like Abdel? Lull had no answer to that.

Nonetheless, appeals for Abdel ben Tajah to come forward appeared on all the local TV stations, and in the newspapers as well. The police claimed they needed him to assist with their inquiries, but I had the feeling that if he turned himself in he would be treated as an accomplice, if not the perpetrator, and I was relieved when the appeals had no effect. If I'd been him, I would have left the city. Perhaps he still had friends in Almería. He could make his way south and lie low. Wait for the whole sordid business to blow over.

Since the press had taken to doorstepping me, camping on the pavement outside my apartment building, I closed my shop and went to stay with Montse and Jaume, who did everything they could to stop me thinking about the impending court case. Montse took a few days off work, and we drove up the coast to the Golf de Roses. We stayed at a hotel she knew, which had a small bay all to itself. We swam two or three times a day, and lay in the autumn sunlight, reading books. One afternoon, we explored the ruins of the ancient city of Empúries, with its wind-softened temple columns and its exquisite and virtually unspoiled floor mosaics, the dark-blue sea in the background, only a few miles away, its surface flecked with white.

Back in Barcelona, we went for walks in the Parc de l'Oreneta and the Parc del Labyrinth. At the weekends we used the mushrooms we had picked in the Collserola to make omelettes and risotto. We sat up late and drank too much red wine. Though Montse was behind me "one hundred percent," there was a night in the kitchen when she looked at me sidelong and said she'd been afraid that something like this might happen.

"Something like this?" I was startled. "You mean you thought someone would get killed?"

Montse smiled and shook her head, then crushed out her cigarette in the ashtray. "Of course not. But you've got to admit, the way you were behaving was extreme—"

"You sound as if you're blaming me."

"I'm not, love. All I'm saying is, I was worried about you." Montse paused. "The whole thing seemed so volatile."

Of all the people who took my side, Mar was by far the most strident. She was back at Bristol, and in her final year, but she called and texted me so regularly that I was never in any doubt as to where her loyalties lay.

"You stood up for your principles," she said on the phone in late October. "You did the right thing."

"But he *died*—"

"And who was the aggressor? Who started it?"

Pol's attitude couldn't have been more different. His discovery that I had been seeing a Moroccan immigrant half my age shocked him even more than the fact that I was implicated in my next-door neighbor's death. He believed I was trying to destroy myself. Kamikaze behavior, he called it.

We met only once during that time, on the Carretera de les Aïgues, an unpaved road that wound its way across the hills at the back of the city. When I pulled up outside the Villa Paula he was already there, sitting behind the wheel of his BMW, and I had the illusion, just for a moment, that I was having an affair with him, and that we were about to have sex, either in my car or in his. I switched off the engine, then rubbed my eyes.

Pol didn't see me approaching—he was so deep in his thoughts, it seemed, that he hadn't heard me arrive—and when I tapped on his window he started so violently that he almost hit his head on the roof. I stepped back, and he opened the door.

"Do you have to creep up on me like that?" he said. "Jesus." He got out of his car and locked it.

"Shall we walk a little?" I said. "Do you have time?"

"I have time." His voice had a sigh in it, and I could imagine him as an old man suddenly, abrupt and querulous. The vision saddened me.

We walked side by side for a while without speaking, though I felt him glancing at me surreptitiously, as if to catch a glimpse of the woman the media were talking about—the woman I'd become...

"How have you been?" I asked.

He laughed a quick dry laugh that came out through his nose.

"I suppose you're angry," I said.

He came to a halt. "Angry?" he said distantly. "Maybe." He looked at me for the first time, and I saw that his face was flushed. "Christ, Amy. I mean, what did you think you were doing?"

"Which part are you talking about?" There was an edge to my voice that I did nothing to disguise.

"Don't be obtuse." He kicked at the road's dusty surface.

The city lay spread out below us, a city I now thought of as my own. I wondered whether Abdel was down there. If so, what would he be doing? Something ordinary, I imagined, like sitting at a table or taking a shower. Or was he in hiding? Had he left the city, after all? I stared at the clutter of pink-and-white buildings as if they might be about to let me know.

"I fell for him," I said, half to myself. "I really fell for him."

Pol looked away again. He seemed to be studying the grass verge. A cyclist in sunglasses and multicolored Lycra fizzed past.

"Is that so strange?" I went on. "You fall for people all the time."

"He was a sex worker, Amy. He went with men."

"He was Moroccan too. You forgot to mention that."

"The way you sound," Pol said, "you'd think it was me who was in the wrong."

I let his words hang on in the air for a few seconds. They were worth thinking about.

"I don't recognize you," he said eventually.

"You never did," I said. "You never did recognize me."

I walked away from him before he could say anything else. I couldn't bear to have him in front of me. He was as bad as all the others. Worse, actually. Because he had loved me once. Because he was supposed to know me. Because he was bound to me by what we had in common—a child. I stopped outside a house that was built on a steep slope in the land, its flat concrete roof on a level with the road. Though it overlooked the whole of the city, it had a feral, run-down feel to it, like a hideout for poachers or thieves. The front door used to be green, but most of the paint had flaked off, and chicken wire had been nailed over the windows. In the garden, which was made up of half a dozen narrow, unwatered terraces, there were bits of rusting machinery and several splintery wooden hutches. I had once seen a dog rooting about down there. With its rangy, muscular body and rheumy eyes, it had looked as wild and neglected as the property itself. I had no idea who the owners or the occupants might be. I must have walked past the house a hundred times, and I had never seen a living soul.

"I'm sorry."

I spun round. I'd forgotten that I wasn't alone.

Pol was considering the ground in front of him, his hands in his pockets, his shoulders rounded, as if he had shrunk into himself. "I'm sorry for everything that happened," he said. "I'm sorry for what went wrong between us."

"I'm sorry too," I said.

"What you were doing—it was reckless."

"So people keep telling me."

"But it's over now..." His eyes lifted, and he looked at me warily.

"Yes."

"And you're all right?"

"Yes," I said. "I'm all right."

He made a sound that wasn't quite a word, then came up close and wrapped me in his arms. I was too astonished to resist. And then I didn't want to. There was the sudden sound of people running towards us along the road. Lots of them.

They seemed in step with each other, their footfalls coinciding, like a Roman cohort moving at full speed. Something was said as they passed by. I heard good-natured laughter. My face was turned to one side, my cheek against Pol's jacket. A green lizard flickered across the flat roof of the house.

"Did you see that?" Pol said.

"See what?"

"Some Barça players just ran past. Players who are injured sometimes train up here in the day." He paused. "Ronaldinho grinned at us."

I stepped back and looked into his face. "Will you visit me when I'm in prison?"

He grasped me by the shoulders and held me at arm's length. There was a lightness around his eyes, and everything poisonous or poisoned dropped away, revealing the outline of whatever it was I'd fallen in love with all those years ago.

"It won't come to that," he said.

THE MOMENT THE TRIAL BEGAN, things went against me. The principal witness for the prosecution was the driver of the car that had struck the deceased. Though he had not been charged, there was a sense in which he was defending himself. He had to make sure that I took all the blame for what had happened. Watching him testify in his dark-blue suit and his sensible brown shoes, I felt shabby, doomed. He told the court that events had unfolded right in front of him, lit up by his headlights. "Like a piece of theater," he said. He was so fluent that I suspected he had been rehearsing. It was even possible that he'd been coached. He had seen two people push an old man into the road, he went on. Though he'd been driving slowly, he'd had no time to react. He identified me as one of those responsible. He said that I hadn't lifted a finger to help. I hadn't called an ambulance, or the police. He'd had to do all that himself. He had also heard me tell my accomplice, Abdel ben Tajah, to leave the scene. My lawyer challenged the use of the word "accomplice." If Mr. ben Tajah was innocent, the driver said, why would he leave? The driver of the second car was able to confirm that Mr. ben Tajah had made a run for it. He didn't run, I told the court later, when I was cross-examined. He walked. There was laughter in the public gallery, which angered the judge. And anyway, I went on, it was me. I was the one who gave Senyor Artes a push. My friend had nothing to do with it. Looking down at her papers, the prosecutor allowed herself a discreet smile, as if I had fallen into a trap she had laid for me. I might have pushed Senyor Artes, I added, but I'd had no intention of pushing him *into the road*. He had staggered backwards. Lost his balance. Senyor Artes assaulted my friend, I said, and I was just trying to protect him. But Abdel was absent, and couldn't corroborate my version of events. The prosecution called several character witnesses for the deceased. It turned out that he had lived his entire life in Sarrià. He had worked as a waiter, then as a lorry driver. Later, he had run a shop that sold wines and spirits. He had even served on the council in a minor capacity. Much to my amazement, everyone seemed to have liked Artes. The worst that could be said of him, a work colleague told the court, was that he could sometimes be a little gruff. *Gruff?* I almost choked.

On the third day, however, the trial took an unexpected turn. My lawyer called a new witness. Baltasar Gallego Magallón. The doors at the back of the court opened, and there was a gasp, as if all the air had been sucked out of the room. The name was unfamiliar to me, but I could hardly fail to recognize the man who stepped into the witness box. His extraordinary height, his old-fashioned hair. The way his knee and ankle joints seemed to need tightening. I would never forget the sight of him emerging from that side street at two-thirty in the morning as I walked home from Montse's house.

Once he had confirmed his name, he was asked to inform the court of his address. He lived on the same street as the defendant, he said, in the building opposite. His apartment was on the third floor, at the front. This came as a complete surprise to me. On meeting him, I had assumed he lived somewhere in Sarrià, but I'd had no idea that he might be my neighbor. I had never so much as caught a glimpse of him, even though it had been almost two years since I'd moved in. But I was missing his testimony.

"...I usually sleep during the day. It's my way of avoiding people." He paused. "I should really be asleep right now."

A murmur of amusement went through the court.

"You say you avoid people," my lawyer said. "Why is that?"

"Didn't you notice the reaction when I walked into the room?"

My lawyer nodded.

"It's what has always happened," Senyor Magallón went on, "ever since I was a child. People pointing and staring—making jokes..."

"But if you only go out at night," my lawyer said, "there are fewer people around, and you attract less attention?"

"Exactly." Magallón glanced at me and smiled faintly, and I knew he was thinking of our chance meeting on Major de Sarrià.

"On the evening in question, you woke at about seven o'clock. Is that correct?"

Magallón nodded. "They're digging up the drains not far from where I live, and the drilling kept me awake. I got up later than usual."

"Did you see the defendant that evening?"

"Yes, I was on my terrace when she left her building. This would have been at about nine o'clock. Her Moroccan friend was with her."

"And did you see them return?"

"I did."

It was close to midnight, he said, and he was sitting by his living-room window, looking down into the street. Unlike the driver of the first car, whose account was partial, at best, he had witnessed the entire incident, from beginning to end. He had seen Senyor Artes step out of the building and light a cigar. Looking to his left, he saw the defendant and her friend approaching. He noticed that the young man seemed to hang back, as if he wanted to avoid a confrontation. He thought he heard the defendant say, "It's my home as well." Words to that effect, anyway. The street was narrow, he explained, with tall apartment buildings on both sides. Voices tended to carry.

When the couple arrived at the entrance to the building, he saw Senyor Artes bar their way. He also heard Artes use abusive language, he said, and this was nothing new. He had witnessed previous altercations between the defendant and the deceased, and had been shocked by the insults the defendant had been exposed to on a regular basis. In fact, he was surprised she had put up with it. If he—Magallón—had been the object of such treatment, he would have complained to the authorities.

My lawyer interrupted. "But on that particular night?"

Magallón looked across at me with somber eyes. On that particular night, he said, he had watched dumbfounded as Senyor Artes launched a completely unprovoked attack on the young Moroccan man, striking him across the face with his walking stick. It was true that the defendant had pushed Artes, but she had been acting in self-defense. After all, he might have struck her next. That night, he seemed capable of anything. The push caught Artes off balance, and he had lost his footing. That was why he had stumbled backwards into the path of the car that happened to be approaching at that moment. There had been no malicious intent on the part of the defendant. The whole thing had been an accident—an unfortunate accident. Magallón paused. In a way, he went on, Senyor Artes only had himself to blame. He, Baltasar Gallego Magallón, didn't wish to speak ill of the dead, but he had never come across such an extreme example of irascibility and prejudice in his entire life—and as a giant, he added, using the word for the first time, and giving it a savage, sardonic twist, he was something of an expert in prejudice.

NOT LONG AFTER the case against me was dropped, I closed my shop for good. I had been acquitted in a court of law—the judge ruled that the death was accidental—but I had slept with a man who was half my age, a man who had worked as a male prostitute, and thanks to the lurid media coverage I had acquired a kind of notoriety that could only damage a business like mine. I gave notice on my apartment and found a new place downtown, in the Raval, where no one knew me and no one cared. It had two tiny bedrooms, and a narrow balcony where I could put my lemon tree and my geraniums, and I was paying less than half what I had paid in Sarrià. I gave my Marquesa plant to Montse and Jaume. Mar told me she preferred the Raval. Though she had liked Sarrià well enough, she had always found it a bit conservative. Quiet too.

"Well, it'll be a whole lot quieter now I'm not there," I said.

She laughed at that.

In January, when I was settled, I went to call on Senyor Magallón. I wanted to thank him for coming to my aid. For saving me, really. It felt strange to turn the corner into my old street, to ignore my own building and enter the one that stood opposite. I climbed the stairs to the third floor. When Magallón answered the door, he didn't seem overly surprised to see me. Inviting me in, he showed me to a table by the window and offered me red wine. I saw that he couldn't stand upright, but had to walk through the small apartment with his head at a slight angle. He noticed me noticing. He dreamed of moving to the first floor, he told me, where the ceilings were higher. A rueful smile came and went on his huge face. It saddened him that I had left the area, he said—he had seen the removals van from his terrace—but at the same time he understood. He asked if I had succeeded in making a new life for myself, and I said that I had, and that it was all thanks to him. He looked at me steadily, then reached for his glass and emptied it.

"I lied," he said.

I met his gaze, but didn't follow.

"In court," he said. "I lied."

Not about the incident itself, he went on, which he had witnessed, as he claimed to have done, but about Senyor Artes constantly insulting me. He didn't know anything about that. He'd made it up.

"Why would you do that?" I said. "Why would you lie?"

"Because I knew you were telling the truth. I knew you were innocent."

I told him he had risked his own freedom—he had committed perjury—but he shrugged and said he had no regrets. He would do the same again, if the opportunity arose. He felt justice had been done. He poured us both a second glass, and we talked of other things.

That spring, I took French classes, and soon became fluent in the language. In time, I was hired by an organization that worked with immigrants from North Africa. Though I had several contacts in the Moroccan community, I chose not to make any inquiries about Abdel. We had been involved in something that had endangered us. It was also more than I could have ever expected, or hoped for. To pursue it would be willful. Greedy. It was enough. I never saw him again, or heard mention of his name. I could only assume that he had moved elsewhere.

Once in a while, after work, I would take the metro up to Sarrià, and I would appear at Baltasar's door with some delicacy I had bought in Foix—he was fond of the pinenut-encrusted marzipan balls known as *panellets*—or with a couple of Styrofoam boxes of *patatas bravas* from Bar Tomás. I would drink a glass of something with him, and later, towards midnight, when the streets had largely emptied of people, we would go for a walk, and I always wondered what local residents made of us if they happened to glance out of their windows as we went past.

THE KING OF CASTELLDEFELS

I'M LYING ON MY BACK in someone's garden. It feels late. My mouth tastes of red wine. Cigarettes. There's a big house behind me. I'm not sure whose it is. Above my head is an umbrella pine, its branches blacker than the sky.

I look down at myself. I'm wearing trousers I've never seen before. With their loud check pattern, they look like they might belong to a golfer, but I don't know anybody who plays golf except a guy I call the dodgy Swede, and he's been away all summer, in Helsinki.

I can hear the trickle of a filter system. There must be a pool nearby.

Where am I?

Everything's floating, flowing. Brain, skin, lawn—it's all the same.

My phone goes off. Tinny little ringtone. That'll be my girlfriend, Cristiani. I let the phone take a message. I just need to lie here for a while.

If I lie here for a while, things'll be okay.

MY NAME is Ignacio Gomez Cabrera—Nacho, to most people—and I've lived in Castelldefels for fifteen years, ever since my marriage ended. It's half an hour southwest of Barcelona, along a strip of oil-stained, down-at-heel motorway. There are clubs with neon signs that crackle on and off, and tall stands of bleached-out pampas grass, and hookers in plastic miniskirts and wrap-around shades who look like they've just been teleported in from outer space. Part dormitory town, part beach resort, Castelldefels has always had its own unique atmosphere, especially at night—a low-level buzz, a foxiness, a slightly sleazy cool. My apartment dates from the 1970s. So does my furniture. Naugahyde armchairs, a teak stereogram. A glass-fronted cocktail cabinet. All original. I'm on the ground floor, three streets back from the Passeig Maritím, and I've got a patio with crazy paving and a kidney-shaped pool with a built-in jacuzzi. It's a good setup.

For the last seven years I've been with Cristiani. I'm sixty-four, she's thirty-nine. I met her in Carinhoso, a Brazilian club not far from where I live. I'd arranged to have a drink with Oriol, a musician friend I hadn't seen for ages. He wasn't there when I arrived, but that didn't surprise me. Oriol was always late—for everything. I was sitting at a table in the corner when a waitress I didn't recognize came over. I ordered a rum-and-Coke, then followed her with my eyes as she moved off. She was wearing metallic-blue high heels. When she had almost reached the bar, she glanced back at me, over one shoulder. Women always know when you're watching them, even if they're not looking. I felt empty, giddy, faintly sick, as if my blood sugar had plummeted.

I asked Emerson about her. Emerson owned the place.

"That's Cristiani." He looked across at her and ran his snaky tongue over his lips. "She's new."

Five minutes later my phone vibrated on the smoked-glass tabletop. It was Oriol. He said he'd been inexplicably delayed.

I lit a Camel. "Do you mean unavoidably, Oriol, or is it something you can't explain?"

He laughed.

"You're not coming, are you," I said.

He told me he was in Terrassa, then called me a few choice names, as if it was all my fault.

Terrassa is about fifty kilometers northwest of Castell-defels, and there's no easy way of getting from one to the other, not unless you have a car, and Oriol, being Oriol, had never bothered learning how to drive. I'd been stood up. But a Chico Buarque song was playing on the sound system and I was being waited on by Cristiani, so I wasn't too put out. I stayed on at the club.

Towards midnight Cristiani took my lighter off the table without asking and lit a cigarette. Narrowing her eyes against the smoke, she stood back, one hand on her hip. "You're pretty stylish, aren't you—for an old guy."

Old guy. I was only fifty-seven then.

"You're pretty stylish yourself," I said. "Those shoes."

She looked down. "You like them?"

"I do. And your feet. I like your feet as well."

"You can't see my feet."

I smiled mysteriously, as if I had X-ray vision or something, then I asked where she was from.

She tapped a few gray flakes into the ashtray. "Brazil."

"Yes, but where?"

"São Luis?" She made it sound like a question because she didn't think I would've heard of it.

"There's an outdoor club in São Luis," I said, "over the bridge. I forget the name of it. I went there once."

"The Bela Vista?" She was so startled and delighted that her face had opened up wide. It wasn't a smile exactly. More like a kind of radiance.

"The Bela Vista. That's it!" Though to be honest I wasn't sure.

"You were in the Bela Vista? I don't believe it. I used to go there when I was, like, sixteen."

I told her about the night I got into a VW Beetle with a guy called João and some of his friends, and how we drove to an apartment block on the far side of the river. We picked our way across a darkened room that was full of people lying on the floor, asleep, and then smoked grass on a tiny balcony, looking out into a warm wild blackness. We were six or seven stories up. There were almost no lights in that part of town, or maybe there had been a brownout. A strong wind blew the smell of mud into our faces. Later, we clattered down the stairs, laughing. When we parked outside the Bela Vista, the driver was so high he couldn't even get out of the car. I went in with João and the others, and we ordered a round of drinks. A live band was playing a song made famous by Gilberto Gil. At some point I went to check on the driver. When I opened the car door, he toppled sideways like a sack of rice. I had to lift him up and wedge him back behind the wheel.

Cristiani was nodding. "I used to know guys like that."

I had been to her hometown, which seemed enough of a basis on which to ask her out, and perhaps because she was still marveling at the coincidence she said yes.

A few nights later I took her to an upmarket seafood place where I was a regular. It turned out that she had been married before, as I had. She didn't say much about her ex, only that he used to deal coke, and that she'd left him while he was doing time in La Modelo for assault and possession of a firearm. He came looking for her the moment he got out, as she had known he would. Men like that, she said, they don't let nothing go, even if they don't want it any more. Makes them look weak. There had been a few nervous years in the mid-nineties, when she didn't answer the phone or the door for fear it might be him, but he was back in Brazil now—Fortaleza, last she heard—and she'd had no news from him in ages. He could be dead for all I know, she said. In fact, I kind of hope he is. She crossed herself, then glanced up through the ceiling to where God sat in judgment. I imagined him shaking his head in exasperation or dismay, and then forgiving her. God always forgave Cristiani. He just couldn't help himself.

When she first mentioned her ex, I felt like backing off—I'd been around some of those characters myself, and I knew how they could set fire to your life—but she swore that he was gone, and I was touched that she cared enough to want to put my mind at rest.

She asked me what I did, as people always do. I chose not to talk about the restaurants I used to own, and my other business interests were too complex to go into. Instead, I told her I was a musician, which was less true, though not a complete lie. As a young man, I'd played piano in a jazz ensemble called the Elsa Slump Quartet. Elsa came from east Tennessee, and she had one of those smoky cracked voices that make you think of neon in the rain at night and love gone wrong. We toured all over Europe, everywhere from Tromsø to Tarifa. We were even booked by the Blue Note in Greenwich Village once. Then, in the mid-seventies, we just sort of drifted apart. These days, when I played, it was usually with friends, after a few drinks, or sometimes I did a residency at one of the big hotels. The clientele wasn't exactly classy—a mix of traveling salesmen, tourist couples with sunburnt shoulders, and husbands cheating on their wives—but at least I could walk home afterwards.

I made Cristiani laugh a lot that night, and when I asked if she fancied a nightcap she leaned across and kissed me on the mouth. Once in my apartment, I opened a bottle of Mount Gay and mixed two Hurricanes while she moved slowly from one room to another and then out through the sliding glass door onto the patio. When I brought her cocktail out to her, she was sitting by the pool, at the deep end, with her feet dangling in the water.

"Have a swim if you like," I said.

She shook her head. "I'm way too drunk. I think I'd drown."

I sat near her, on a lounger.

After a while, she looked back through the picture window. "It's a lot of space," she said, "for just one guy."

I smiled, but didn't say a word.

Back indoors, she asked me to play something, and I had a stab at "All the Things You Are," my favorite Dave Brubeck track. I was drunk too, and I messed it up, but Cristiani didn't notice. Later, she told me she'd been mesmerized by the way my fingers moved over the keys. Made her feel horny, she said.

When I woke the next day, the bathroom door was open and Cristiani was bent over the toilet in a pair of pale-green knickers, being sick. It was one of the most beautiful things I'd ever seen.

"What did you do to me?" she murmured.

Afterwards, she lay across the crumpled sheets with a dishcloth full of ice cubes on her forehead. She swore in weak, husky Portuguese that she would never touch dark rum again.

Three months later, she was living in my apartment.

WHEN CRISTIANI MOVED IN, her seven-year-old son, Aristides, came with her, like one of those supermarket deals where you get a free mug with a wedge of Parmesan. I already had two children of my own, and I didn't particularly want any more. I certainly didn't want evidence of Cristiani's shady past shoved in my face twenty-four hours a day—Ari was the child she'd had with the trigger-happy drug dealer—but what could I do? It was either both of them or nothing. During the time I had lived as a bachelor, I had fallen into the habit of spending my weekend mornings in a local bar called Bang Bang. I would have a few beers and catch up on the gossip with Pepe, the guy who ran the place. Some women would have tried to change me. Not Cristiani. On the first Saturday, when I told her I was going out, she just said she'd see me in a couple of hours, for lunch, confirming something I'd already guessed about her: she would let me be myself. I was so relieved I asked if she'd like me to take Ari.

"Sure," she said. "You guys go to the bar."

It became a ritual. Every Saturday, I would leave the apartment with Ari at about eleven. I taught him how to order drinks and how to get me cigarettes from the machine, but he spent most of his time by the window reading comics, a glass of Coke fizzing at his elbow. I would walk over now and then and ask if he needed anything—another soft drink? more crisps?—and he would smile, as if touched by my attentiveness.

Once, when I checked on him, I found him flipping through that day's edition of *Mundo Deportivo*.

"You like football?" I said.

He looked up at me. "Doesn't everyone?"

I hadn't showed the slightest interest in sport before, not even as a boy. I had never understood what people got so worked up about. I knew there was an intense rivalry between the city's two football teams, FC Barcelona and Espanyol, but it was Ari who taught me the difference between them. He gave me potted histories of the clubs, including their political affiliations, and then described the current squads, player by player. His conclusion was that we should support FC Barcelona—it was richer, and more successful—unless, of course, I had a fondness for the underdog.

"No," I said. "Barça it is."

I approved of his thorough, almost intellectual approach, and in the back of my mind there lurked the thought that Cristiani would love me all the more if I appeared to be bonding with her son.

On our first visit to the Camp Nou, we watched Barça play Real Mallorca in the league. It was early in the season, a regular Sunday evening in October, but as Ari said on the drive into the city—and this was typical of him—it was better to start quietly and then build up. All the same, when we walked into that deep well of a stadium, with the watered, floodlit green of the pitch below us and the full moon trapped in a neat circle of evening sky above, I don't know which one of us was the more excited. Cristiani had called us her "two men" as she said goodbye to us, but we were more like a couple of kids, and as the weeks passed I began to look forward to arriving in Barcelona on a match night—the streets packed with fans on motorbikes, the scratchy feel of a ten-euro Barça scarf around my neck, the hot dogs with fried onions at halftime...

Towards the end of that first game, I nudged Ari in the ribs. "I want to thank you."

He peered at me through his glasses. "For what?"

"You brought me here." Looking around, I opened my hands. "Without you, none of this would've happened."

In the summer of 2003 FC Barcelona signed Ronaldinho from Paris Saint-Germain. He was already world famous by then, thanks partly to the spectacular forty-yard free kick he had scored against England in the World Cup quarterfinals the year before. Ari's reaction to the news was muted. He was troubled by Ronaldinho's tricks, and by his lack of consistency. He worried the Brazilian star was a show pony, and might not adapt to Barça's style.

For as long as I could remember there had been a Brazilian community in Castelldefels, so it didn't surprise me when I heard that Ronaldinho had bought a mansion in Las Heras, an exclusive neighborhood in the hills above the town.

Ronnie.

There was no one in Barcelona who didn't know his name. He was more or less the first person you saw when you flew into the city. As you left the airport, passing the Estrella beer factory, there was a giant billboard with Ronnie on it, brandishing a packet of sugar-free gum—Ronnie with his glistening braids tied back in a ponytail, Ronnie with his infectious, bucktoothed grin...

One Saturday morning, about eighteen months after he had signed for Barça, I set out for the bar, as usual. Ari had a fever that day, and he had stayed at home, in bed. I'd just stopped at a junction to light a cigarette when a big silver

SUV pulled up next to me. I looked round, and there was Ronnie, his eyes shielded by designer shades, reggaeton blasting through the half-open window. A diamond the size of a chick pea glittered in his ear.

"Ronnie!" I had to raise my voice to make myself heard over the music. "You're a legend."

He showed me those famous fucked-up teeth of his.

I remember Barça were playing at home the following evening, a game I would watch on TV with Ari, if he felt well enough.

"Good luck tomorrow," I shouted.

Still grinning, Ronnie gave me a thumbs-up, then drove away.

What passed between us during those few, seemingly inconsequential seconds is difficult to describe. There was a current, certainly. A kind of connection.

When I let myself into the apartment two hours later, the heated-up remains of the previous night's *feijoada* was already on the table, and Cristiani was standing at the sink, washing her hands. She was wearing a short skirt made of a stretchy, tight-fitting material, and her feet were bare. The cherry varnish on her toenails was chipped but vivid. It looked as if she had the hangover I should've had, a hangover I'd headed off with half a dozen *cañas* and the odd crafty belt of whiskey.

"That smells great," I said as I fetched a bottle of Cabernet Sauvignon and a corkscrew.

"You're in a good mood," she said, not looking round.

"You know why?"

"Because you're drunk again?"

Cristiani had a vicious streak that always made me want to hug her. I felt quickened by her sharpness.

"As it happens," I said, pouring us both a glass of mellow red, "I just met Ronaldinho."

She turned to face me. "You're kidding, right?"

I smiled. "I'm not kidding."

Once we sat down to eat, I filled her in on my encounter with Ronnie, and how I had felt something pass between us.

"Strange you should see him first," she said. "Emerson told me he showed up at the club."

Cristiani still waitressed at Carinhoso now and then, if Emerson needed helping out. He'd always had a soft spot for her. It was Emerson who had bought her those metallic-blue high heels, though she swore blind that nothing had ever happened between them. She could never go with a man like that, she said. He looked like a pimp. She'd feel dirty. But you let him buy you a pair of shoes, I wanted to say. You gave him a foot in the door, so to speak. I kept quiet, though, knowing that if I seemed to be finding fault it would light a touchpaper in her. I didn't bring up her convict of a husband either. If she felt the urge to rewrite her life story, that was fine by me. Maybe that was why she'd chosen me, so she could erase some old unhappy version of herself. And it was true that Emerson looked like a pimp. He wore his hair long, even though he was going bald—it snaggled over his collar in limp, oily ringlets—and he always left the top five or six buttons of his shirt undone so everybody could admire the slew of gold medallions that hung between his pumped-up pectorals. Cristiani once said it looked as if someone had dumped a whole pile of loose change on his chest, which made me laugh at the time. Later, I wondered if she hadn't given herself away. To come up with an image like that, wouldn't you have to see the person naked, and lying down?

I shifted in my chair and hooked an arm around her. The waist of a seventeen-year-old, I'd always told her. You'd never have guessed she'd had a child. She stared through the picture window, her wineglass halfway to her mouth.

I smiled. "So you haven't seen Ronaldinho yet?"

She shook her head.

"You will," I said.

She was still looking out over the patio. "It's spring already. We really ought to clean that pool."

IT WAS ARI who gave me my nickname. One Saturday in February we left the apartment together, strolling side by side. The sky was hard and blue, as it often is during the winter, and the breeze had an edge of iron to it, a subtle hint of snow. Sometimes you can smell the Pyrenees, even though they're more than two hundred kilometers away. That morning I happened to run into a number of friends and acquaintances along the way, and a walk that would normally have taken five minutes took half an hour.

As we finally approached the bar, Ari squinted at me through his glasses. "You know a lot of people, don't you."

"Well, I've lived here for quite a while."

"But you know everyone."

"Not *everyone*." Though I felt oddly flattered that he should think so.

He nodded. "You're like a king."

I stopped and looked at him.

"The King of Castelldefels," he said.

"I like that." I took out my packet of Camels and gestured with my lighter. "The king lights up."

Ari grinned. "The king has his first cigarette of the day."

"Third, actually," I said.

I ruffled his hair, then we turned and walked into the bar, both of us chuckling.

By then, I had grown to love Ari like a son, though I was still mystified by the extent to which he failed to resemble his mother. In photographs taken when she was Ari's age, Cristiani was dark and slender, almost undernourished. She'd had big eyes, like a waif. Ari, by contrast, had pallid skin and a physique that was doughy, unathletic. Her hair was wavy, his was straight. He wore glasses, which gave him an air that was scholarly, intense. She had never read a book in her life. Where did his looks come from? His father, presumably. Every once in a while, I would search his face for an echo of Cristiani, some nuance I had missed, and he would catch me at it and ask why I was staring. In time, though, I began to find the fact that they seemed unrelated reassuring. My love for Ari had nothing to do with the love I felt for Cristiani. It had happened naturally, of its own accord. It was unforced, honest. Pure.

I HAVE ALWAYS been lucky with money. Not long after I met Montse, the woman I would marry, I stopped playing the piano and went into partnership with Ferran, someone I'd known during my last two years at school. We opened a *chiringuito*—a beach bar—in Castelldefels, one of the first, and it did well from the beginning, especially at weekends, when people drove down from the city. Over the years, the bar expanded and became a fully fledged restaurant. Later, we opened a second restaurant, in the town center. When Montse kicked me out in 1988, I sold my share of the business to pay alimony and maintenance—we had two daughters, Beatriz and Imma, who were still very young—but I invested the leftover cash in another of Ferran's schemes, a property development on the Costa Brava. The timing couldn't have been better. Back then, the coast was booming, with hordes of British and German tourists looking for cheap holidays in the sun, and I had survived on the proceeds ever since. The girls were both grown up now, and they had jobs and partners of their own, so my overheads had dwindled. My investments were still paying off, though. I had plenty in the bank, enough to give Cristiani and Ari pretty much whatever they wanted.

WHEN CARINHOSO CELEBRATED its twenty-fifth anniversary in June 2006, I gathered a few people together—some Catalan friends, a couple of Brazilians, the dodgy Swede, and Vic, a guy from London. We had been at the club for about an hour, and I was up at the bar with Vic, ordering drinks, when he nudged my shoulder, then tilted his head towards the entrance.

"Ronaldinho," he said.

My heart did a kind of somersault. I hadn't seen Ronaldinho since the morning he pulled up next to me in his silver SUV. I wasn't the only person to react. Everybody did. The air itself seemed to shift and tighten. Suddenly we all knew we were in exactly the right place. How often does that happen? In the season that had just come to an end, Barça had retained La Liga, and had also won the Champions' League, and Ronnie had been central to the team's success, scoring twenty-six goals in all competitions, including two against our bitter rivals, Real Madrid. Even Ari's concerns had been laid to rest.

Ronnie was wearing a diamond-studded crucifix, a platinum R10 medallion, and a gem-encrusted watch the size of an apple, but his skin looked even more expensive than his jewelry. In fact, his whole being looked expensive. I'm not sure what it is about celebrities, but they appear to glow. Is it something we invest them with, or do they actually give off light? And if they do give off light, could it be the residue of all that flash photography, all those fascinated glances? I managed to catch his eye as he moved past, and he gave me a puzzled look, as if he couldn't quite place me. It was hardly surprising. Think of all the people he must have met.

"I saw you about a year ago," I told him, "on the street. It was the day before you scored that second-minute goal against La Coruña. You were in your SUV."

"Right." His face cleared, and he was grinning, just like the billboard outside the airport. "You're the guy who was having trouble lighting his cigarette."

"Trouble? What trouble?"

"The old hand was shaking a bit. Probably all those drinks you'd had the night before."

He was still grinning, and I was grinning too, though I didn't have a clue what he was on about. I replayed the scene. There I was, standing at the junction in my light-brown suit and my eggshell-colored shirt, an unsparked Camel between my lips, when Ronnie pulled up in his fuck-off spaceship of a vehicle. I produced my lighter and ran my thumb over the little corrugated metal wheel, dipping my head downwards to meet the flame, then lifting my head again and releasing the first plume of smoke into the sunlit air without touching the cigarette at all. It would have looked like one fluid action, controlled and graceful, right down to the way I pocketed the lighter afterwards. It even had a certain sleight-of-hand about it, as if, in my working life, I was actually a conjuror or a magician. As for shaking, I wasn't shaking at all. I wasn't even trembling. *The king lights up*. I looked at Ronnie again and realized he was taking the mickey. It was strange, but I'd never imagined that he might be funny—somehow you don't expect famous people to have a sense of humor—and the discovery delighted me. I gave him a playful punch on the shoulder and felt my knuckles bounce off a dome of muscle.

"How would you know I was shaking, anyway?" I said.

"I was looking right at you, *cabrón*."

I laughed. "You were wearing those two-thousand-dollar shades of yours. You probably couldn't see a thing."

One of his bodyguards leaned down and murmured in his ear.

"Come to think of it," I went on, "should you really have been driving?"

When I returned to my table, Emerson was sprawled on the banquette next to Cristiani. His ganja-sleepy, slightly reptilian gaze strolled across her breasts, which rose temptingly out of her scoop-neck Custo T-shirt. A young blond woman sat on the other side of him. She wore an off-the-shoulder dress that looked like it was made of scrunched-up golden tissue paper. The dodgy Swede was regaling her with tales of his heroics on the golf course—last time out, he'd shot a hole-in-one, apparently—but she didn't appear to be listening. Emerson bumped fists with me as I dropped into the narrow gap between him and Cristiani. I put my arm round her and leaned back. Bossa nova pulsed through the purple leatherette.

"You forgot the drinks," Cristiani said.

I smiled at my absentmindedness. "Sorry, love. I was having a word with Ronnie."

"Ronnie?"

"Ronaldinho."

"He's here?" She looked past me, into the crush of people. "I don't see him."

"That's because he's got an entourage with him. Bodyguards and all that. They're even bigger than he is." I told her how Ronnie had remembered me, and how I'd been wrongfooted by his sense of humor. "I wasn't expecting it. You don't, do you—not from a footballer."

"He *remembered* you? From when?"

"That time I met him on the street. I told you."

She shook her head. "You're the one with the sense of humor, Nacho. You're a funny guy."

I kissed her neck.

"What about that drink?" she said.

I handed her a fifty-euro note. "Can you go?"

As Cristiani moved away, I turned and spoke to Emerson. "Ronnie's here."

"Yeah?"

"I just talked to him. He's over by the bar."

Emerson nodded slowly. "It's not the first time he's been in."

I had heard Emerson brag about his club to anyone who'd listen—he was even proud of the walls, with their cheesy, garish murals of the beach at Copacabana—and I knew his blasé response was a cover for the bolt of gratification that had jolted through him like a speedball or a hit of crack.

He disentangled himself from the blond girl. "I guess I should go over." Uncoiling up onto his feet, like a cobra rising from its basket, he adjusted his sheer black shirt so it lay flush against his torso. Through the rayon or viscose or whatever-the-fuck slithery fabric it was made of, I could detect the swellings and ripples he'd acquired during endless, mindless hours in the gym. He reached up with both hands, his thumbs at right angles to the rest of his fingers, and smoothed the straggling strands of hair away from his forehead, back behind his ears, then he eased forwards, into the crowd.

Cristiani returned with the drinks.

"You know, I don't blame Emerson," I said.

"For what?"

"For trying it on with you. You're gorgeous."

She took my left hand and pushed her lips into the palm, and I could feel her tongue tracing the lines, especially the one that curled past the base of my thumb, then she wedged that same hand between her thighs and, leaning over, gently bit one of my nipples through my shirt. Brazilian girls. Jesus.

"No one's talking to me," the blond girl said.

As if on cue, the guy from London came over and sat down next to her. He asked if she could act.

"I've done some modeling," she said.

"You want to be in a movie?"

"Sure." She picked up her cocktail and took the straw between her lips. Her cheeks hollowed as she drank.

"You make movies, Vic?" I said.

He turned to me, and I saw that his pupils were dilated.

"Me?" he said. "I do all kinds of things."

Later, I saw Ronnie again. He had taken off his shirt and he was dancing with two girls, his moves poised, hydraulic. We didn't get another chance to talk, but he acknowledged me from a distance, one eye closing and opening again in slow motion.

It was after four when we got home, and I went straight to bed, but Cristiani said she wasn't tired. I wondered if she would call Brazil. She usually did when she'd been drinking. It would be midnight in São Luis. Her mother would still be up. She'd be sitting in front of her tiny 13-inch TV, the picture fuzzy and washed out, like a window display that has seen too much sun. Cristiani, are you crazy? she would say. This must be costing you a fortune. Then they'd talk nonstop for half an hour. Or if her mother didn't answer there was always her good-for-nothing brother, who worked for the post office in Recife. He would weigh tourists' letters and charge them for the stamps. When the tourists had gone, he would put the stamps back, toss the letters away, and pocket the money. He was more than doubling his salary. These days, though, thanks to advances in technology, people were writing fewer letters. Pretty soon he'd have to find another scam. As my head sank down onto the pillow, I heard Cristiani uncork a bottle. She was the kind of woman people take one look at and say, *I don't know where she puts it all*. There was a clatter as ice cubes tumbled out of the dispenser on the fridge. Most of them would miss her glass. Go skidding across the kitchen floor. I imagined them melting, half a dozen little pools of water in the dark, and then, just before sleep took me, the stereo started up, pumping out the first bouncy chords of one of her favorite reggae CDs from Salvador Bahía.

I HAD AN AFFAIR with Elsa Slump. I was living in Vienna then. We all were. When Elsa was naked, she looked like a sculpture by Giacometti. High conical breasts. Thin tapering legs. Long feet. Her skin so black it had a bluish tinge to it. She reminded me of something pulled from a blaze, all charred wood and a lick of blue flame round the edges. I would show up at her apartment to find her wandering about in a cream silk robe she'd bought in the flea market, hugging the points of her elbows and muttering to herself. She drank whiskey for breakfast and kept goldfish in every room. If the water tilted in their bowls, she would know an earthquake was happening. They don't have earthquakes in Vienna, I told her. Baby, she said in her dehydrated voice, there's always a first time. Before she went to sleep, she would soak a bath towel in the sink and lay it on the floor next to the bed in case the building caught fire in the night and she needed to escape. She left the lights on too. She had the habit of sleeping in her shoes. She would take them off to make love, then put them on again afterwards. Some people smoke after they've had sex. Elsa put her shoes back on.

Drugs and alcohol: they brought us together, and kept us together—for a while, anyway. Elsa carried a leather-coated hip flask everywhere with her. Inside was the opium tea she bought from a young aristocratic type who claimed he was also an arms dealer. His name was Florian. Strange I should remember that. And I remember a party in a building out near the Ring, one vast room after another, and double doors so tall you could've ridden through the apartment on a horse. Elsa rolled a joint as big as the trumpets that brought down the walls of Jericho. It took an age to smoke. Later, she massaged the fingers of my left hand with such focus and intensity that I began to feel off balance, like a seesaw with a fat man sitting on one end. Then I was sprawled across her bed with a half-empty bottle of schnapps, and her with nothing on—someone must have given us a lift or else we walked—and her skin glowed all over, except for her heels and elbows, which were dusty gray and rough as pumice, and I moved away from her mouth, which tasted of summer even though it was snowing outside, and as I kissed her throat I became aware of a flicker on the sideboard, by the wall, a goldfish darting but the water steady, no earthquakes happening that night, and I wondered if goldfish ever slept, and if so, did they lie on the bottom of their glass bowls or did they float on the surface, and did they close their eyes? The glare from the naked bulb pushed into every angle and crevice of that drafty room. It seemed a bright transparent box had dropped from somewhere high above, a box made to slot perfectly into the space. Elsa pushed my face away from her breasts, they were too sensitive, and when she came, a humming or keening spilled out of her, a kind of talking, but all mixed up and unintelligible, as if she was speaking in tongues. Hairs prickled at the apex of my spine, and I blacked out. The next day I asked what she'd said, but she had no memory of saying anything at all. She thought I was the crazy one—hearing voices, as she put it, and lying in the middle of the road to make a taxi stop. Did I do that? I said. She forced me to feel the back of my coat, still damp from all the melted snow. I never saw no one get as stoned as you, she said. Later, when there was no longer anything between us, people told me she was schizophrenic, but everyone I knew had problems of one sort or another, and Elsa didn't seem different enough to have earned a special label of her own. She was just Elsa.

We lasted several months, and though we were never in love our two lives or the way we looked at things seemed eerily aligned. Huddled under a pile of blankets on a winter morning, we would notice the shape of a car edging along the top of the orange cloth she had draped over the window in place of a curtain, some kind of shadow or reflection from outside, and we would marvel at how small the car was, like a toy, or we would be sitting over a *grosser brauner* in our local café and the door would swing open, cold air gusting, and we would look up to see a bearded man in a green hunting jacket and we'd both know, and know it with certainty and in the very same instant, that he had poisoned his wife and got away with it. There were moments during live performances—in Paris or Cologne or Amsterdam—when I would chance on harmonic progressions or melodic lines that rode along with her voice, and her eyes would meet mine across the sparkly half-darkness up onstage, amusement on her face, and a gentle pity, and even, sometimes, a glimmer of mockery or malice, at the thought that I might have the nerve to follow her, because she knew she could sing herself right out of where she stood, she could leave me for dust if she wanted to.

IT WAS MY HABIT, most evenings, to go for a walk. I would start near the yacht club and head off down the beach, into the setting sun, only turning round when I reached the final *chiringuito*. In its width and bleakness, the beach looked Dutch, though the Dutch beaches I had known were scoured by fierce winds and backed onto low dunes and tufts of marram grass, memories of Sunday outings with Elsa, the two of us in long black overcoats and sunglasses. In Castelldefels, I carried a pair of old espadrilles, and made sure I had Camels in my jacket pocket. I liked how they tasted when I smoked them by the sea.

One evening at the end of 2006, only a few months after the party at Carinhoso, I saw a familiar figure jogging towards me, his ponytail swishing from side to side. Dressed in a white baseball shirt and baggy white shorts, he was running barefoot on the firm damp sand, just out of reach of the waves. He was on his own, which surprised me. Somehow I had imagined that he was so valuable and so much in demand that he would be constantly surrounded, even while he slept.

When he noticed me, he slowed to a walk. A low sun shone over my shoulder, into his face. He wore his two-carat diamond ear studs, as usual, and his signature R10 medallion. Like a racehorse, he was handicapped—with jewelry. As the distance between us closed, I was struck by how vivid he was. It was as if he was differently constructed than the rest of us, more densely pixelated. He filled the space he occupied to the very limit. He pushed his own envelope. Physically, of course, but also spiritually. Esoterically. For that reason, perhaps, he seemed—I don't know—bigger. I wondered which had come first, the charisma or the fame.

He clasped my hand. "Hey Nacho, you're laughing."

"I'm just happy to see you, Ronnie," I said. "I don't know what it is. You carry some kind of charge around with you. I feel it. The city feels it too. It's glad you're here."

He looked beyond me, into the setting sun. He might have been jogging, but he hadn't even broken sweat. "You want to go for a run?" He was trying not to grin. With Ronnie, a grin was never far away.

I lit a cigarette. "I'm sixty-something. It would probably kill me."

"And that won't?" He gestured at my cigarette.

"Your Spanish is coming along nicely."

He moved past me, and I turned and walked with him, back the way I had come, my cigarette in one hand, my shoes in the other.

"Shouldn't you keep going?" I said. "I don't want to hold you up."

"I already did two training sessions, at La Masia."

"Are you feeling good about Sunday?"

He nodded. "What you just said about my Spanish—"

"I meant it."

"No, I need to improve. My accent's terrible."

Bending down, I pressed my cigarette butt into the sand. I was tempted to tell him that he really should be learning Catalan—he was in Catalunya, after all—but this was Ronaldinho I was dealing with, so I bit my tongue.

"I'd be happy to help you out," I said.

"Some conversation would be good," he said. "You know, everyday stuff. Football, music—girls..."

He eased his toes under an abandoned Styrofoam coffee cup, balanced it on top of his foot, then flicked it up onto his forehead. It was magical, what he could do. But there was nobody anywhere nearby. Nobody saw. It must be strange for him, I thought, to be performing with an audience of one. No roar of the crowd, no rapturous chanting of his name . . . Perhaps it made a change, though. Perhaps it came as a relief. Time out. Or perhaps it was all connected, the private and the public, everything flowing from the horn of plenty that was his genius.

"You think you could do that, *caballero*?" His face was parallel with the sky, the Styrofoam cup resting, rim down, on his forehead. "You think you could talk to me now and then?" With a jerk of his neck muscles, he flipped the cup into the air and volleyed it right-footed into an approaching wave, then he looked heavenwards with both arms raised and the middle fingers of each hand tucked into his palms, as he always did when he scored a goal, and I suddenly saw how young he was, younger even than my daughters, almost still a boy.

"When do you want to start?" I said.

He lowered his arms. "Come over to the house. We'll have a barbecue. Are you free next Tuesday?"

"Tuesday?" I pretended to be thinking. "I don't know, Ronnie. I'll have to see if I can fit it into my busy schedule."

My wife Montse divorced me because she thought I was having an affair. Appearing without warning at the restaurant one afternoon, she found me sitting on the terrace with a waitress called Carmen. I was holding Carmen's hand and talking to her in a low murmur. I wanted her to remember what I was saying, and I didn't want anybody else to overhear. Carmen was a beauty—dark-blond hair, dark-brown eyes—but she had rejected my advances not long after

I hired her, only to be dumped a few months later by her racing-driver boyfriend, and on the afternoon in question I was trying to comfort her, with no hidden agenda of my own, my attentiveness heightened by the slightly sadistic pleasure I was taking in the fact that she was suffering. I don't know how long Montse watched us for. Long enough, in any case, to see what she'd expected to see. Long enough to have her suspicions confirmed.

"I knew it," she said as she stepped onto the terrace.

"Montse? What are you doing here?" I turned to Carmen. "Carmen, this is Montse. My wife."

Carmen stared up at her, swollen-eyed.

"Nice to meet you," Montse said. "Now get lost."

As Carmen ran back into the restaurant—she handed in her notice that same afternoon—I rose to my feet, lifting my arms away from my sides. "Montse, it's not what you—"

"It's not what I what?"

I sighed.

"I've had it up to here," she said, "with your pathetic adolescent fucking around."

People were beginning to stare.

The irony was, I was guilty—in general, at least. I had been unfaithful to Montse throughout our marriage, though not, as it happened, in the previous six months. Wiser then to focus on the specific charge, of which I was, sad to say, entirely innocent.

"Montse," I said, managing to muster a little outrage, "there's absolutely nothing going on between me and Carmen. She's an em—"

"You think I'm a fool?" Montse said. "I know what I walked in on." Her voice was scornful, withering. "You were telling her it's over. That's why she's upset."

She was so sure she was right and at the same time so wide of the mark that I had to laugh.

"All you walked in on," I said, "was your own insecurity."

Not a bad line, given I'd thought of it there and then.

Montse snatched up the ashtray and hurled it at me. A slurry of crushed butts, ash, and rainwater slid down the front of my white linen shirt. She stalked away, her long hair swinging like a soft pendulum against the small of her back, her legs taut and tanned.

"You know what your problem is?" she said, looking at me across one shoulder as she unlocked her jeep. "You're a drunk."

I pointed at the table where I'd been sitting. An empty coffee cup and Carmen's can of Diet Coke. "I don't see any alcohol."

"Try looking in your bloodstream, fuckwit."

The jeep roared away, back wheels spinning on the beige dirt of the restaurant car park.

Montse changed the locks that week, while I was at work, and I had to look for somewhere else to live. Though Beatriz and Imma were only four and two and a half, respectively, they were old enough to realize that something was broken, and they mourned its loss. I mourned it too. I couldn't believe Montse was serious, and kept trying to persuade her that she was making a mistake, but she wouldn't relent, not even for the sake of the girls. I had betrayed her, and she wanted to "cut my heart out," as she told me more than once. She would never be able to trust me again. After two years, I stopped sending her *pedres brunes* from Foix and orchids from the garden center in Pedralbes. I also stopped taking her calls when her jeep wouldn't start or when her income tax needed sorting out. I had done my utmost to win her back, and I had failed. It was time to turn away. Get on with my life. More than a decade had passed since I had touched a piano, but I bought a Yamaha DX7 secondhand and began to play again. I decided to make a study of Keith Jarrett—his technique had always impressed me—and I quickly grew to relish evenings spent in the apartment I rented round the corner from my old house. I would sit at my Yamaha in nothing but a pair of boxer shorts with the windows open and a bottle of wine or whiskey at my elbow, going over and over a piece called "Lalene."

By the time Montse showed signs of wanting me back, it was too late. I had started dating Monica, a graphic designer in her thirties. Then it was Rosa. Then Mercé. I wasn't with anyone for very long, which only confirmed Montse's low opinion of me. I was faithless. Superficial. I was "a fucking butterfly." So far as Beatriz and Imma were concerned, though, I lived on my own. I never introduced them to any of my girlfriends—not until Cristiani, that is. And you can imagine what Montse had to say about her. "Led by the balls" was one of her less provocative remarks. Well, yes. Obviously. But there was more to it than that. Cristiani didn't try to force me to be something I didn't want to be. There was no second-guessing involved, and no need for compromise. No sense that I might be letting her down. If I felt like staying out till four in the morning, that was fine with her. If I felt like staying home and watching TV, that was also fine.

To Montse's surprise—and chagrin too, no doubt—Beatriz and Imma took to Cristiani right away. It would have been hard not to. She dressed them in flamboyant costumes and put on impromptu fashion shows. She taught them to cook Brazilian specialities like *feijoada* and *moqueça*. She transformed the patio into an outdoor nightclub—the Bela Vista!—with nonalcoholic cocktails and strings of colored lightbulbs, and the three of them would dance to *bumba meu boi* records from São Luis. Sometimes Ari would act as DJ or bartender. He was a few years younger than my daughters, and they liked to mother him and spoil him. They had always wanted a little brother, they said. First I'd heard of it, but still. There was I, thinking they would hate me, and that I would be constantly having to take sides or smooth ruffled feathers. Nothing of the kind. We all got on famously—for three or four years, anyway.

ONE SATURDAY in November 2006 I knocked on Ari's door, as usual.

"It's almost eleven," I called through the painted wood.

There was no reply.

I opened the door. Ari was sitting on the edge of his bed with a magazine about BMX bikes open on his lap. He was staring at it so hard that I knew he wasn't seeing it at all. It was just a way of not looking at me.

I kept my voice gentle, calm. "It's time to go to the bar."

"I'm not coming," he muttered.

"What's wrong? Are you ill?"

Without lifting his head, he shot me a fast, surly look that seemed to come from just below his eyebrows. "Do I look ill?"

I went to the window. It was a beautiful morning. I could already imagine how the light would fall in a bright wedge across the floor of the bar, and how the first gulp of beer would fizz down my parched throat.

"Guess who I saw the other day."

Ari didn't say anything, but I felt the curiosity rising out of him despite himself, like a genie.

"I was walking along the beach," I went on, "as I often do in the evening, and who should come jogging along the sand but Ronaldinho."

Ari shook his head. "That's ridiculous."

"There he was, like magic, right in front of me. He had this hip-hop outfit on—I don't suppose 'outfit' is the right word—and he was wearing that medallion he always wears—you know, the one that says R10—"

"You're making this up."

"We started talking. He sort of teased me about going for a run." I chuckled. "He seemed really friendly. You know—approachable. Wants me to give him Spanish lessons—"

"*Spanish* lessons?"

"He needs to work on his accent. He thinks I can help."

"Why would he talk to you?"

"I'm the king," I said, "remember?"

Ari gave me a different look this time, one of thinly veiled contempt. "It never happened."

I had a strange slow feeling, as though my life force was ebbing away, and for a moment or two I thought I might pass out. Was it hypoglycemia? Or had I eaten something that disagreed with me? Then I realized what it was. My love for Ari was draining out of me, and I knew it would be hard to replenish or recapture. I felt emptier than I had in years. Worse still, I could hear Elsa singing in my head, her phrasing sluggish, sinister. Shoes on a table, broken mirror. One magpie on its own...

I turned away. "Well, if you don't believe me—"

All of a sudden, Ari's bike mag was splayed on the floor like a shot bird, and he was on his feet, shouting. "No, I don't. I *don't* believe you. You're *lying*."

I backed out of his room and closed the door.

In the kitchen, Cristiani was making juice. "What was all that about?" She tossed a hollowed-out half-orange in the bin.

"I asked Ari if he was coming to the bar, and he started shouting at me." I paused. "I don't know what's got into him."

She looked at me over her shoulder, then reached for another orange and cut it decisively in half.

ELSA WAS FOUND DEAD in a Marseille hotel, aged thirty-seven. On hearing the news, I drove up the coast with Dave Brubeck's *Time Further Out* on the car stereo. I had told

Montse an old friend of mine had died, though I didn't mention that it was a woman, or that we had once been lovers. I said I'd be away for a day or two, no more.

By the time I arrived, the police had taken over, and since I wasn't a member of Elsa's family I wasn't allowed to see the body. But her family's in America, I said. Even as I spoke, it struck me that Elsa had never talked about her family at all. She viewed herself as a stand-alone, with no roots, no antecedents. I was her family, I told the police. I performed with her. This outburst seemed to puzzle them. Maybe it was my garbled French, or maybe they hadn't expected me to start crying. I hadn't expected it myself. She was a singer, I went on, dabbing my eyes. A great singer, actually. They asked me who I was. I played piano in her band, I told them. I went out with her too—for a while. They asked if I knew about the drugs. Of course, I said. We were musicians. They smiled bleakly. And then, just when it seemed they might relax the rules and let me see her after all, I told them I had changed my mind. I'd found Elsa strung out enough times to know what that might look like. I left the police station and stood on the pavement outside. Loud gulls wheeled overhead. The air smelled of fried fish. Though I had given up cigarettes, I bought a packet of Disque Bleu and chain-smoked three.

Built out of pale-yellow stucco, with black wrought-iron balconies, the Hotel Bellevue looked out over Marseille's Vieux-Port. The man behind reception had black hair and colorless lips, and his ears lay flush against his head, as if they had been pinned or glued. I asked if I could have five minutes in the room where Miss Slump had died—I was a close friend, I told him—but he said it was a crime scene. It had been cordoned off. How much was it worth to him? I asked. Five hundred francs? A thousand? Adopting a haughty look, as if he had never done anything wrong in his entire life, let alone accepted a bribe, he moved his head slowly from side to side. I felt like hitting him in that pale mouth of his. I felt like twisting those perfect little ears. Trying to keep my voice even, I asked if he had seen her. That slow shaking of the head again. He hadn't been on duty when she checked in. I asked how many nights she'd stayed. Just the one, he said. I turned towards the window. So there's really nothing you can tell me? I said. Nothing at all? Something about the rare deep blue of the sea, and no one knowing who Elsa was—no one knowing, or even caring... There were tears in my eyes again. The whole view wobbled.

"She was in bed when they found her," the man said suddenly.

I nodded. That was how I'd imagined it.

"She had her shoes on."

"That's her," I said. "That's Elsa." I thought I heard the man stifle a laugh, and I swung round. "What's wrong with that?"

He shrugged.

Some lines from a song she'd written came back to me. *He told me I was hollow / He said I was empty inside / It was so cold he wrapped me in his coat / I laughed / I cried / I whispered in his ear / If you ain't hollow / How are you supposed to float?*

On my return to Barcelona, I tried to locate Elsa's family—the Slumps of Tennessee—but the Internet didn't exist back then, and I got nowhere. Elsa was buried in Marseille, among strangers. I paid for a stone, and had it engraved with the words I'd remembered as I stood in the lobby of the Hotel Bellevue. Some weeks later, the French police sent me her few remaining possessions. That was almost the saddest part of the story, the fact that I was the only person she had left. The smell of summer was gone from her clothes, wiped out by something institutional like bleach or camphor. I had no use for any of her things—I gave them to a local charity—though I kept the shoes she'd died in. They brought back a time in my life that was so remote and skewed that it seemed like part of someone else's.

RONNIE'S HOUSE didn't disappoint me. Screened by a mature umbrella pine and a high stone wall topped with lavish sprays of bougainvillea, it wasn't visible from the road. Once I'd been buzzed in through an electronic metal gate, I walked up a drive, past a row of gleaming cars. A maid in a black-and-white uniform was waiting for me. She led me through a series of cool dark rooms, the walls hung with folk art and musical instruments. Towards the rear, the house opened out into a living area that had the biggest sofas I had ever seen. Two people could lie facing each other, and their feet wouldn't even touch. Beyond the living area were a paved terrace and a lawn. A blue pool glittered in the sun. Sprawled on a lounger, Ronnie had a phone pressed to his ear. As I stepped outside, he passed the phone to a man in a light-gray summer suit who was sitting beneath a huge white-and-orange beach umbrella. I recognized him from the sports pages. It was Ronnie's brother, Roberto Assis, who also acted as his agent. Beyond the men, on the lush cropped grass, were two girls in micro-bikinis. They lay on their backs with their eyes closed, earbuds in their ears. Their oiled bodies shone like glass.

When Ronnie saw me, he grinned and told me to take a seat. His brother leaned over and shook my hand, just in case I was somebody who mattered, then he stood up and buttoned his jacket.

"Think it over, Ronnie," he said. "I'll call you later."

They embraced quickly.

"You like the place?" Ronnie asked when his brother had gone.

"What's not to like?" I let my gaze drift towards the trees at the back of the property. Their leaves stirred lazily. "Your family must be very happy here."

Ronnie nodded. "Everyone's happy." But his dark eyes had misted over.

"Are you thinking about your father?"

"How did you guess?"

I shrugged.

Ronnie's father used to work in the shipyard in Porto Alegre. He had died of a heart attack when Ronnie was just eight years old.

"I'll never get over him passing away like that. It left a hole that can't be filled." He looked round at the house, the pool, the girls. "Not by this. Not by anything."

"He'd be very proud of you."

"You think?"

"I'm sure of it."

Ronnie gave me a strange look, both his eyes half-closed. "Sometimes I get the feeling we've met before."

"Really? Where?"

"I don't know. Another life, maybe."

"You believe in all that?"

"Why not?" And there was his grin again—natural, open, utterly infectious.

Growing up near Brazil's southern border, Ronnie would probably have been exposed to Candomblé Ketu, a religion which, for me, bore more than a passing resemblance to voodoo, since it relied on ritual sacrifice, hypnotic drumming, and trance states. Among my friends, I've always been seen as a bit of a skeptic. They talk about my arching eyebrows and the jaundiced lines around my mouth. I even look like a skeptic. In the presence of Ronnie's grin, though, my skepticism seemed out of place. Beside the point. If Ronnie thought we had known each other before, that was good enough for me. And Ronnie, being Ronnie, was used to people listening to him. Agreeing with what he said. His whole existence revolved around his intuitions. You only had to watch him play to know how in tune he was, how connected with the universe. His eyes would go one way, and the ball would squirt off somewhere else. He specialized in a kind of *sombrero*—or lob—that left opponents facing in the wrong direction, and looking stupid, while he moved smoothly away across the pitch. One touch from him and the game changed gear. Things clicked, things flowed. He was the stitching in the fabric, the oil in the machinery. So I chose to accept his version of events. If nothing else, it explained the feeling of familiarity I'd had when I first saw him. It also had the effect of binding us together still more closely.

Later, we worked on his pronunciation—especially his *h*'s, which were far too soft. The sound he needed to make, I told him, was harsh and aspirated. Think of a man clearing his throat before he spits. I demonstrated once or twice, and Ronnie copied me. One of the girls opened her eyes and squinted at us, a bewildered look on her beautiful blank face, and me and Ronnie grinned at each other.

Me and Ronnie.

WHEN I WOKE the next day, Cristiani was already up. Judging by the position of the sun on the bedroom floor, it was noon. I closed my eyes, hoping to doze off again. There was a hissing in my ears, as if I'd been listening to loud music, and my brain was rolling about in my skull, soft and clumsy, like a plastic bag full of water.

An hour passed.

Finally, I hauled myself out of bed and went into the living room. Cristiani was over by the picture window. She was just standing there, staring at the crazy paving. Light bounced off the pool, outlining her in gold. I sat down on the sofa. The apartment seemed quieter than usual. No radio playing, no TV. She turned to face me, leaning against the wall with her arms folded. I noticed a red mark and a slight swelling near her left eye. When she was drunk, she often bumped into things.

I asked her how she was.

She looked past me, towards the kitchen. "Where did you get to last night?"

"I was at Ronnie's house. We were working on his accent. After that, it all gets kind of vague."

"You made quite a speech," she said, "when you came home."

I searched around inside my head for an inkling of what I might have said, but there was nothing there.

"You don't remember?"

"Sort of," I said. "What was it about?"

"It was about how much you love me, and how special I am. Apparently, I'm the only person who understands you."

"Sounds like I went on a bit."

"You did. You went on for half an hour." She paused. "Then you wanted sex."

"How did that go?" I said lightly, trying not to sound as if I didn't have the faintest idea.

"Not so good."

"Oh." Just then, I felt blood surge to the place where it should probably have been the night before. "That speech I made, though. It was true."

She was looking at me quizzically, almost warily, as if she suspected me of trying to deceive her.

"Really," I said. "It was."

She lowered her eyes. "If you say so."

"Where's Ari?"

"He went out."

"Come here a minute."

She didn't move.

I got up off the sofa and walked over. When I was close to her, I put my fingers gently to her chin and lifted it so I could see her face. "How did you get that bruise?"

One Monday in late June, Cristiani took the car and drove up the coast with Ari. School had finished, and she was planning to spend a few days with a friend of hers who owned a house in Tossa de Mar. I had a lot going on, I told her, but maybe I could join them at the weekend. I didn't need to come at all, she said, not if I was busy, and she widened her eyes as she always did if she was trying to convince me of something, or if she was being sincere. I used to love that look. Over the years, some of the shine has worn off. It's just not in the nature of things to keep gleaming when they're no longer new.

On Friday, clouds started piling up in the northwest, and by the evening it was raining hard. I was sitting at home, watching old black-and-white footage of the Elsa Slump Quartet, when the bell rang. Someone was at the gate. I went to the front door and peered out, but the rain was torrential. I couldn't see a thing. Thinking it must be one of my drinking partners from the bar—they knew I was on my own—I pressed the buzzer and the gate clicked open. To my surprise, Ronnie loped across the yard towards me.

He stood in my hallway, dripping. "Crazy weather."

I brought him a towel.

"You got any dry clothes?" he said.

"In *your* size?"

He grinned, but there was something swollen or misshapen about his face that told me he wasn't feeling good. There had been problems at the football club, with Ronnie supposedly responsible for confrontations in the dressing room. Stories about his fluctuating weight and poor attendance at training sessions kept appearing in the sports pages. *Ronaldinho's in the gym* had become a running joke.

I fetched him a pale-blue fleece and a pair of tracksuit pants. When he had changed, I took his wet clothes and put them in the dryer. Walking back into the lounge, I found him sitting in one of my armchairs with the towel wrapped round his head.

He stood up and did a twirl. "How do I look?"

I had to laugh at the sight of Ronnie in my clothes. The fleece came down to just below his ribs, and the tracksuit pants were skin-tight. "You look like a million dollars," I said. Which, come to think of it, was probably only a fraction of his worth. "Can I get you something?"

"Is that a caipirinha?" He had noticed the lime segments in my glass.

I nodded.

"One of those," he said. "But you'd better make it weak."

He followed me out to the kitchen where I set to work on a pitcher of caipirinhas. While I chopped the limes and crushed the ice, he moved restlessly round the room. He didn't seem to feel uncomfortable or out of place in my apartment. He had been brought up in far worse surroundings, of course—in a *favela* in Porto Alegre. Every now and then, he stopped at my elbow to check on my technique, but he was never still for very long.

"*Hombre,*" he said, "you really know what you're doing."

"My girlfriend's Brazilian," I told him.

"That's right. I forgot."

I reached for the *cachaça*. "So Ronnie," I said casually, "I don't suppose you came all the way over here in the rain just to work on your Spanish."

He gave me a calculating look from under his eyebrows, his chin lowered, as if he was about to take a free kick twenty-five yards from goal. "My mother's left for Brazil."

"I think I read about that in the papers." I poured a drink and handed it to him. "She'll be back," I said, "won't she."

He nodded, then sipped his drink. I asked him what he thought.

"Good," he said. "Not exactly weak, though."

"One won't hurt."

"She left at the beginning of the month. My brother too. The house feels kind of empty."

"No girlfriends?"

"It's not the same."

"Well, I'm always here, if you need me."

"Thanks, *amigo.*" He put his glass down on the work surface. "Sometimes the silence really gets to me."

"I know that silence."

I led him back to the lounge. Outside, it was still raining hard. The patio lights were on, and the pool looked like a bed of nails.

Ronnie's eyes were drawn to the TV. "What are you watching?"

"It's some footage of the jazz band I was in."

"You were in a band?"

"This is us performing live in Hamburg. I'm not sure what year it was. Nineteen-seventy, I think—or it might have been '71." A thought struck me, and I shook my head. "You weren't even born yet."

Ronnie sat down and leaned forwards, his forearms resting on his knees, hands dangling. At that moment the camera panned across the stage to the piano.

"Nacho," he said. "Is that you?"

"That's me."

"You weren't bad-looking, were you—for a Spaniard."

"Ronnie," I said, "I'm Catalan."

But he was quiet, just watching. Maybe the footage had taken him out of himself—temporarily, at least. If you were Ronaldinho, nobody ever let you forget it. The price he paid for all that wealth and fame was to be condemned to that one version of himself. In me, though, he had found a way of escaping. I freed him up. He was even wearing my clothes!

"That singer," he murmured. "Spooky."

I told him the story of our affair, then took him into my bedroom to show him Elsa's shoes, which I kept in a box frame on the wall. I had never explained their significance to anyone, not even Cristiani. Ronnie was the first. You could run from an earthquake or a fire, I said. You could run from your childhood, your family. Your past. But you couldn't run from death. Death would take you when it chose—shoes or no shoes.

Ronnie was standing so close to the box frame that his breath clouded the glass, and he didn't move for a long time. Was he thinking, once again, about his father? Or was he thinking about the moment when he would have to hang up his boots? At last, he turned away and looked at me. His face was somber, grave. "Would you play something for me, Nacho?"

"I'm a bit rusty," I said, "but I'll give it a go."

Back in the lounge I switched on my electric piano, and Ronnie settled in an armchair. I asked if he'd heard of Keith Jarrett. He hadn't.

"This is something he used to play a lot," I said. "It's called 'Lalene.'"

The first note dropped into the silence in the room like the ever-widening, ring-shaped ripple that happens when you lob a stone into a pond. A second note came soon after. Then a third. In no time at all, I was drawn into the darkness deep inside myself. When I approached a piece with the right degree of intensity, it always seemed to me that outer space was nothing compared to the space that was to be found in my own head. I saw myself as infinite—*on the inside.* And music was the craft or vessel that allowed me to explore that universe...

I played on.

I inhabited "Lalene" so thoroughly that night that I was able to move in all directions. I expanded on the piece. I improvised. I went to places I hadn't known existed. When I finally lifted my fingers off the keys and looked around I saw that I was quite alone.

"Ronnie?"

I stood up and walked out to the kitchen. The jug of caipirinhas I had made was empty, as were three bottles of wine, and a pan of spaghetti carbonara had spilled down the front of the gas stove and onto the floor. My sunglasses lay in a mass of congealed pasta, their arms reaching blindly upwards, as if asking for help. Ronnie must've got hungry while I was playing. You could tell he didn't cook too often. He'd probably have people to do that for him, of course. To clear up after him as well, judging by the state of the kitchen. What'd he been doing with my sunglasses, though?

I went into the bedroom, thinking he might be taking another look at Elsa's shoes, but he wasn't there. He wasn't on the patio either, or in the pool. I checked the bathroom. His clothes had disappeared from the dryer, and the towel I had given him was screwed up on the floor. There was no sign of the pale-blue fleece or the tracksuit pants. He must still be wearing them. I opened my front door and went out to the gate. His SUV was nowhere to be seen. Strange that he'd left without a word—it wasn't like him—but then it occurred to me that I might have been so wrapped up in the Jarrett piece that I hadn't heard him say goodbye. Or perhaps he hadn't wanted to interrupt me, out of respect. He could be sensitive that way. Or maybe, embarrassed by the mess he had made, he had slipped quietly out into the dark... The rain had moved inland, over the hills. Wet leaves gleamed. I glanced at my watch and was astonished to see that it was almost half past four. I had been playing for at least three hours.

Fierce sunlight woke me. It was after midday. If I didn't hurry, I would miss my session at the bar. Luckily, I had gone to sleep in my clothes, so there was no need to get dressed. I didn't have time to wash or shave. Running the hot tap in the kitchen, I cleaned the egg and bacon off my sunglasses, then I put them on, picked up my wallet and keys, and left the apartment.

I was halfway across the yard when somebody called my name. It was Maite, the forty-something divorcee who lived upstairs. She was wearing a blouse with multicolored squares all over it. Without my shades, it would have hurt to look at her.

"You were making a lot of noise last night," she said. "I couldn't sleep."

"Sorry. A friend came over."

"Only one? It sounded like a party."

"Did the music bother you?"

"The breaking glass bothered me. The yelling bothered me. I don't remember any music."

"My friend"—I shook my head fondly, despairingly—"he thought he'd try and cook spaghetti—"

"Didn't you hear me banging on the ceiling?"

I thought hard. "No, I don't think I heard anything like that."

"I was using a broomstick. I was pounding on the floor." Maite paused. "It's got dents in it now."

"A broomstick?"

"What about when I came to the door? It was two-thirty in the morning."

"I was lost in the music—in a kind of trance. I've been working on this piece by Keith—"

"I knocked and knocked. You didn't answer."

"You know something, Maite? You need to relax a bit. Chill out."

"That's easy for you to say. You don't have to work." She turned away, and then turned back again. "Next time, I'm calling the police, okay?"

"I like your blouse. Is that new?"

She put her hands on her hips, but I thought I could see the beginning of a smile on her face. "You're a real pain in the ass, Mr. Cabrera."

It was another five minutes before I could get away. Some people just talk and talk. I suppose she was lonely—like Ronnie. By the time I got to the bar, it was quarter past one.

Pepe looked up from the newspaper that lay open on the bar. "You're late today."

"I was up half the night, practicing a new piece. On the piano."

"I don't think I've ever heard you play."

"Give me a *caña,* would you?"

Pepe held the glass at a slant under a silver tap, adjusting it as it filled with beer, then he deftly scraped the foam off with a plastic knife. It was always a pleasure to see him go about his trade. You could feel the years of experience in every action, no matter how small or insignificant.

He asked where Ari was.

"He's up the coast," I said, "with Cristiani." I drained half the beer, then sighed with pleasure and lit a cigarette. The smoke turned from gray to blue as it coiled through a ray of sun.

"How is Cristiani? I haven't seen her in a while."

I tapped my Camel against the edge of the ashtray. "She's fine. She's visiting a friend, in Tossa."

"Are they away for long?"

"I suppose it depends on the weather. It's been nice up there, apparently." I slid my empty glass towards him and watched it fill with beer again. The scene that lay before me—the bottles lined up in their neat rows against the mirror-tiled back wall, the sunlight slanting in—was bright and colorful but thin somehow, like a fabric that might tear. All of a sudden, I wasn't sure how long Cristiani had been gone.

"You going to join them?" Pepe asked.

"I might."

He glanced at me, and then away again. "Nice-looking woman like that."

I stubbed out my cigarette, then studied him for a moment. "What are you trying to say?"

"It's none of my business." Pepe rinsed out a rag and wiped the counter, even though the counter was already clean.

A silence fell.

Then Sergio, another regular, pushed through the door and tapped his thumb on the side of his forefinger, the signal we all used to tell Pepe to activate the cigarette machine.

First Maite, now Pepe. What'd got into everyone?

THAT EVENING, the phone rang. By the time I found it, stuffed down the side of the armchair Ronnie had been sitting in, the ringing had stopped. It was Cristiani, and she had left a message saying she'd decided to stay in Tossa for another week or two. She sounded distracted, remote—not like herself at all. When I called her back, it went straight to voicemail. I tried again. Same thing. I could only think there wasn't too much cover where she was.

The next morning, on a whim, I asked Pepe if I could borrow his car. I wanted to drive up to Tossa and surprise Cristiani.

"It's only for the day," I said. "I'll take her shopping, then we'll have dinner. I'll be back before midnight."

"The window on the driver's side is stuck—"

"I thought you fixed that—"

"And the air-con doesn't work, not unless you turn it up to maximum."

"All right."

"Don't go over a hundred. The whole thing starts to shake."

"You're beginning to sound like my mother."

Pepe gave me a look, then put his car keys on the counter.

"And don't drive drunk," he called after me as I headed for the door.

Once on the *carretera,* I opened the window on the passenger's side, but the air that blew into the car seemed hotter than the air I was already breathing. In the distance, to the northwest, the foothills of the Pyrenees showed up gray-white in the heat haze. Feeling drowsy, I took a nip of brandy from the bottle I'd stowed in the glove compartment. What bothered me was that I couldn't remember Cristiani leaving for Tossa. I had no memory of her packing a bag or saying goodbye, no memory of me standing on the street outside our apartment, waving. And yet the car was gone, and so was she. Had I been there when she left? If not, where *had* I been?

I turned off the A7 towards the Costa Brava, passing through Tordera, then circling the seaside town of Blanes. After Lloret de Mar, the road began to climb, curve after curve, the pine trees and aloe vera closing in. Sharp brown rocks tumbled steeply to a Mediterranean that looked almost purple. The sky had darkened, and I heard thunder, even above the mumbling and rattling of Pepe's beaten-up old SEAT. I sped over a ridge and down a long straight stretch of road, passing a grilled-meat place, then I swung round one or two more bends, and there was Tossa, wedged between two headlands, with its fairy-tale castle and its high-backed, dun-colored church. I remembered the life-size bronze statue of Ava Gardner that overlooked the bay. Not long after the war, she had made a movie in Tossa, and the townspeople had never forgotten her. The air had fallen still, an ominous, unsustainable stillness, like a big man hiding in a cupboard, and as I rounded the roundabout with the octopus sculpture on it a crooked vein of silver showed up in the sky to the east. The thunder that burst right above the roof was so loud that I ducked. My knuckles whitened on the steering wheel.

When I reached the narrow street where Cristiani's friend lived, I saw my own car parked at an angle, one tire on the pavement. Cristiani had passed her driving test at the fourth attempt. Sometimes I wondered if she should have passed at all. I tucked Pepe's SEAT into a small space farther up the hill, near the Hotel Neptune, then I walked back down. The storm had cleared the streets. Nothing moved except a three-legged cat that was picking its way along the top of a wall. My knees ached after the drive, but I was feeling lucid. Confident. This surprise appearance was exactly what was called for. It was a demonstration of my love. It would show I cared.

I knocked on the front door just as the first fat drop of rain came down. There was no answer. I knocked again. This time the door opened, and Aristides stood in the gap. He seemed to have grown since I'd last seen him. How old was he now? Fourteen? Since I was standing up against the door, trying to stay dry, my face was close to his, and I felt I was seeing his father, the coke dealer, before me, the man I had always feared but never known. This new insight caught me off guard and robbed me of all the words that I'd prepared on the way up.

"What do you want?" he said.

I noticed he no longer used my name, and I had the feeling this had been going on for quite some time. All the same, I smiled.

"Is that any way to address the king?"

Ari scowled.

Behind me, I could hear the rain landing on parked cars. The sudden smell of wet dust plunged me back into my childhood, and for a few vertiginous moments I was younger than the boy who stood in front of me.

"I'm here to see your mother," I said.

Ari leaned his right hand on the door frame so his arm was blocking my path. "She doesn't want to see you. She's had enough."

"What?"

"You heard."

Adolescents, I thought. Honestly. Though he did frighten me a little, with his brutal, unformed face and his sketchy new mustache and sideburns.

I reached out and fingered the fake gold pendant he was wearing. "What did you get this for? It's crap."

He pushed my hand away and glared at me.

"Where's Cristiani?" I said.

"I'm not saying."

"Is she here?"

He sniffed the air in front of my face and then recoiled. "I thought as much. You're drunk."

"Oh, for Christ's sake—" I knocked his arm aside and shoved my way past him, into the house.

Cristiani was in the back room, sitting at a pine table. The sliding glass door behind her opened onto a narrow, tiled terrace. There was a mop and bucket, a coiled hosepipe, and a blue plastic washing line with clothes hanging out to dry. Though it was raining, no one had thought to bring the washing in.

"Where's your friend?" I said.

She looked at me but didn't speak. She was wearing a tan skirt, a white T-shirt, and open-toed, wedge-heeled shoes. The bruising around her eye had faded. The sight of her chipped scarlet toenails brought a lump to my throat.

"I drove all the way from Castelldefels," I told her. "I had to see you."

I felt heroic, like a knight in a legend. I had proved my loyalty and passion, simply by appearing in Tossa. All this despite the presence of her son, the brutish gatekeeper, who lurked behind me. The air in the room gusted, and I thought I could smell his socks.

"Whose house is this?"

I looked around for clues. The room had the perfect, deadening neutrality of a holiday rental. The glass coffee table with its obligatory conch shell, the dog-eared thrillers on the bookshelf. The modest boxlike TV. Nothing actually belonged to anyone. It was just stuff.

I reached for Cristiani's arm. "I'll take you back with me. You can't stay here."

She made no attempt to get to her feet. I stood beside her, bending from the waist, as if to hear what she might say. But she still hadn't spoken. She hadn't said a word since I'd arrived. Could it be that she was overwhelmed?

"Come on," I said. "I'll take you home."

"Leave her alone!"

I had forgotten about the boy. Tightening my grip on Cristiani's arm, I whirled around. "Stay out of this. It's got nothing—"

He came towards me fast, his hand closed into a fist. I heard a cry. Then the world shrank, until all I could see was that shell on the table—the polished, speckled curve of it, the ridges where it opened in a lip.

I WOKE UP ON MY BACK, rain splashing onto my face. My upper body was on the pavement, but my legs were in the gutter. The hard edge of the curb pressed against my spine. My jacket had been pulled half off, and my shirt had lost two of its buttons. I could see part of my stomach. Its softness and pallor sent a thrill of fear through me.

I sat up. The rain tapped on my skull, making a mockery of my thin hair. My cheek throbbed. When I touched the place where it hurt, there was no blood, only an egglike swelling. There was a sound in my head like the sound you used to get on TV after the channels closed down—but channels don't close down anymore, do they. They just go on and on, dozens and dozens of them, right round the fucking clock.

The house was behind me, and I had the sense that they'd gone out. I imagined the two of them stepping over me, my girlfriend and her pale thug of a son. Once again, I thought I could smell his feet, and this time I saw a color too, a smooth, slightly oily slab of yellow. I leaned sideways and retched, but nothing came up.

I got to my feet, feeling I was made of several large pieces that were barely held together. An old man walked along the pavement towards me, the shoulders of his light summer jacket dark from the downpour, a green plastic bag in one hand. He stopped and stared at me, his head wobbling a little.

"So you got caught in it as well."

Like an oracle, his words seemed rich with meaning.

I climbed back up the hill. It felt much steeper than before, and I had to stop three or four times to rest. When at last I reached Pepe's car, I pulled out the half-empty bottle of brandy from under the passenger seat, unscrewed the metal cap, and took a few swift gulps. The world sprang back into position. I took off my jacket and my shirt, which were both wet, and threw them on the back seat, then I got behind the wheel and slammed the door.

As I passed the house, I sounded the horn three times—I'm not sure why—then I drove on towards the octopus roundabout. Tourists plodded down the main street in flip-flops and cagoules. The shops were open. All those boogie boards and blow-up whales. All those postcards, curling at the edges, damp. I took another nip of brandy, to keep the despondency at bay.

On the way out of Tossa, I switched on the radio and found a music station that was playing Herbie Hancock. I didn't much care for jazz fusion, but I left it on. Clouds hid the tops of the hills. Everything was dark green and soft swirling gray. I could almost have been in Japan. Somewhere oriental, anyway. The fast, intricate music helped me to negotiate the countless bends, and before too long I was dipping down into Lloret again, with its 24-hour discos and its 500-room hotels.

At Blanes, I turned inland. A stud farm, a row of dripping poplars. The last time I had taken the country road between Sant Pere and Hostalric I had been with Vic, the guy from London. He'd had some business on the coast, and I'd gone along for the ride. That day, we must have seen at least half a dozen hookers sitting on white plastic chairs in outsize sunglasses and thigh-length boots. They looked out of place on that deserted road, under the pines. They looked too vivid. To my surprise, Vic stopped on a curve and told me he would be five minutes. I had to wait in his fancy black Lexus while he took one of the girls off into the trees. Today, there was no sign of them. They must have heard the weather forecast and stayed indoors. As I joined the A7, I finished off the brandy. I didn't want to think about what had happened in Tossa. I needed to focus on the job in hand: getting home.

Somehow I missed the exit for the Ronda Litoral, which cut through Barcelona by following the coast. It didn't matter. The Ronda de Dalt would do just as well. As I veered to the left, heading for the west side of the city, I flicked through the stations until I found a song I knew, then I sang along with it as loudly as I could.

I HAD JUST PASSED the turning for Sant Cugat when I noticed a blue light whirling in my rearview mirror. How long had that been there? The police car swerved into the middle lane and drew alongside, the officer in the passenger seat pointing beyond me, signaling that I should take the next exit. I sped up a steep ramp to a roundabout and parked as soon as I could, on a narrow road that led off into the trees above the Ronda. Since the window didn't work, I opened the door and waited. The police pulled in behind me. Two officers got out. The one who approached me had a big round head, with all the features squashed into the middle. I was amazed by how much of his face was blank. The other policeman was circling the car.

"Could you turn the music down?" said the one with the big round head.

I did as he asked.

"We've been following you for three kilometers," he said.

"I didn't notice," I said. "I was in a world of my own."

"Have you been drinking?"

"I had a few nips of brandy, just to warm up." I wondered where the bottle was. On the floor, hopefully. Out of sight.

"You were cold?" the policeman said.

"I got caught in the rain, back in Tossa de Mar."

"Is that why you've got no clothes on?"

"Yes."

I looked where he was looking. The empty brandy bottle was lying in full view, on the passenger seat.

"You look like you've been in a fight," the policeman said.

I touched the swelling on my cheek. "This? It happened last night, in my kitchen. I was cooking spaghetti."

"Eventful life." The voice came from behind me, making me jump. I'd forgotten about the second policeman.

"Step out of the car," the first policeman said, "and get dressed."

I did as I was told. The two officers watched gravely as I buttoned my shirt. It seemed to take forever.

"Still damp, is it?" said the policeman with the big round head.

I nodded. "It is a bit, yes."

"It'll soon dry out."

He was young enough to be my son, and yet his behavior struck me as avuncular—he really seemed to care about me—and I felt a surge of hope. Perhaps there would be a few moments of reprieve in this otherwise relentless day.

They weren't traffic police, he said, and they didn't carry a Breathalyzer, so what he proposed was this: either I accompany them to the nearest police station, which was just down the hill, in Sarrià, or else I could leave the car where it was and pick it up in the morning.

"Your second proposition sounds more agreeable," I said.

The policeman nodded approvingly. It was clear that if he'd been in my predicament he would've come to the same conclusion. "Where do you live?"

"Castelldefels."

"Call a taxi and go home."

"I'll do that."

"Do you have a phone?"

"I do." Reaching into the map pocket in the car, I took out my mobile and waggled it in the air. "And thank you, officer. I appreciate it."

As the two policemen walked back to their car, I pretended to punch a number, then I put my phone to my ear and began to pace up and down, like a zoo animal. It's what people do when they're talking on their phones. I've seen them.

"I'd like a taxi," I said. "I'm just off the Ronda de Dalt. Exit 9."

There was no one on the other end, but I sounded so convincing that I wondered if I'd missed my calling. Could I have been an actor?

I was still talking and gesturing when the police executed a neat three-point turn and drove away. My phone pressed to my ear, I gave them what I hoped was a respectful and law-abiding wave. As they disappeared round the roundabout, I slipped my phone into my trouser pocket and walked onto the bridge that overlooked the Ronda. I watched the cars slide, one by one, into the wide dark mouth of the tunnel. A taxi to Castelldefels would cost me at least fifty euros. As if that wasn't bad enough, I'd have to come back in the morning. Such a bore. My eyes drifted across to Pepe's scruffy red SEAT. Now the police had gone, there was nothing to stop me getting back in the car, was there? I mean, who would ever know? I would drive with—what was the phrase they used?—"due care and attention," taking only the smallest roads. I would meander through Pedralbes, Cornella, and Electricitat, only rejoining the *carretera* when I was past the airport…

I moved cautiously towards the car, as if it was a bomb that might explode. I put my hand on the door handle. It was warm. I looked this way and that, but there was nobody about. Only a deserted car park, a modern building that seemed to be part of a university, and the tunnel's air filters, which rose out of the nearby shrubbery, reminding me of the funnels on an ocean liner. I was in an area called Can Caralleu. I had the feeling I'd been there before, when I was still with Montse. A children's party, perhaps—or a dinner with people I no longer knew. In fact, didn't Montse live somewhere close by with her second husband, that pretentious intellectual, Jaume? In the distance, I heard the eerie piped notes knife grinders use to advertise their presence. Moments later, he appeared on an ancient powder-blue Vespa, his grindstone strapped to the back. I opened the car door and got behind the wheel. If the two policemen returned to check on me, I would tell them I'd felt tired and a little faint, and that I'd decided to wait in the car until my taxi arrived. No harm in that, surely.

I sat quietly, not moving. The sun had almost set. A maid who looked Peruvian walked past.

The traffic on the Ronda lulled me…

I woke suddenly, with my face pressed against the steering wheel. I could feel its curved imprint on my cheek, and my neck was so stiff I could hardly turn my head. Darkness all around. I lifted my right arm so my watch came into view. Hours had gone by. My mouth was dry, but I had nothing left to drink. With a furtive glance in the rearview mirror, to make certain no police were lurking, I pulled the door shut, turned the key in the ignition, and drove off along the winding, hidden road that ran above the Ronda.

IT WAS ALMOST ONE in the morning by the time I opened my front door, and I ached all over. Had Aristides actually hit me? If not, what had caused the swelling under my eye? Even if he wasn't responsible, and I'd sustained the injury in some other way, he must have dragged me out of the house. To think that he left me lying in the gutter like that. The gutter. How could Cristiani have allowed such a thing? Maybe Ari frightened her, just as his father—her drug-dealing ex—had frightened her. I saw him standing in the doorway with his two-bit hip-hop jewelry and his bum fluff. I would never be able to look at him again without thinking of the man who I had never met.

As I dropped my keys into a bowl in the hall, a murmur came from the lounge, and my heart jumped beneath my ribs.

"Cristiani?"

Had she got back before me?

I clicked the lounge light on. Ronnie was stretched out on my sofa, his forearm draped over his eyes. His feet were bare. A pair of Lebron James signature trainers lay on the floor nearby.

"Nacho? Is that you?"

"Jesus, Ronnie, you gave me a fright. I could've had a heart attack. I could've keeled over right there, by the front door."

"You told me I could call by any time. You gave me a key, remember? When I saw you weren't here, I let myself in."

"I thought you were in Brazil."

"I got back Friday. Thought I'd come and see my old friend." He sat up and yawned, then looked at me for the first time. "What happened to you?"

"You should see the other guy."

Ronnie grinned.

I sank into an armchair. The ceiling seemed to lower itself half a meter, like a lift dropping in its shaft. "Did you bring my clothes back?"

"What clothes?"

"The clothes you borrowed the other night."

"Sorry, *caballero*. I forgot."

"It's all right." I didn't blame him. People as rich as he was didn't tend to know the value of things.

"Nacho, would you make me a caipirinha?"

"Sure. I could do with one myself."

I stood up and went out to the kitchen. Ronnie padded after me, his footsteps soft and heavy. I switched on the fluorescent strip light, which pinged and flickered and then stayed on. Since no trace of the spaghetti carbonara remained—the cleaner must have been—I decided not to mention it. No point upsetting him.

"I've got something to tell you," Ronnie said. "Can you keep a secret?"

"Of course." I opened the fridge and took out four limes.

"I've signed for AC Milan."

It had been a difficult season for Ronnie—he didn't see eye to eye with the new manager, Pep Guardiola—and the papers were constantly speculating about his future. There had been a flirtation with Manchester City, and talk of a move to

Italy as well, but nothing concrete had emerged. Now the man himself had confirmed it, though, I felt such a profound sense of abandonment that I stood quite motionless, the fridge door still ajar. I stared at the empty white shelves, then I lowered my eyes and stared at the limes in my hand. The glossy dark-green fruit seemed like the embodiment of melancholy.

"You're one of the first to know," Ronnie said.

I suppose I should've felt flattered, but all I could think of was that I was losing my close friend. I reached for the sharp knife I always used for quartering the limes.

"You'll like Milan," I said.

"You think?"

I tried to inject some enthusiasm into my voice. "It's very stylish. Full of beautiful people." I didn't tell him how cold and gray the winters were—I'd played there one January, with Elsa's band—and presumably he already knew about the lack of beaches.

"It's less money than Manchester, but Berlusconi really wanted me—and I know people in the team. Pato's there—and Kaká..." Ronnie was studying the kitchen floor. "We'll keep in touch."

"My girlfriend's left me," I said.

"I never trusted her."

I swung round. "Really?"

"Careful with that knife!"

"Sorry. It's just—I think she was my last chance—"

"Don't be so gloomy, *amigo*. There are plenty more fish in the sea."

"I don't know, Ronnie. I just don't know."

He poured two drinks and put one down in front of me. "You have to remember who you are." He raised his glass. "To the King of Castelldefels!"

"Who told you about that?" I said.

"Your boy. Ari."

We both drank, then I toasted Ronnie's new life in Milan. The caipirinhas kicked in, and my mind began to soar, taking my whole body with it.

"How *is* Ari?" Ronnie asked. "You haven't mentioned him recently."

"We've not been getting on."

I told Ronnie about the first time Ari said he wasn't coming to the bar. Later that day, I found the dishwasher wrenched loose from the wall, and smashed crockery all over the kitchen floor. The evidence of violence had come as a shock to me.

"You should try and talk to him," Ronnie said. "Kids that age, you have to make an effort. Be patient."

I remembered what had happened in Tossa and shook my head. Then I refilled our glasses. Ronnie was drumming on the Formica work surface with an egg whisk and the wrong end of a spatula. The fact that he was famous always made me feel as if I was younger than he was, but then he would do or say something that brought it home to me that I was old enough to be his grandfather.

"Watch this," he said.

Scooping a red Fuji apple off the kitchen table with his right foot, he flicked it up onto his knee, where he bounced it four or five times before flipping it onto his left shoulder and rolling it slowly over the back of his neck. There was a moment of absolute stillness, then his right shoulder twitched, lobbing the apple high into the air, and as it came down he volleyed it right-footed through the kitchen window, which just happened to be open, and I heard it thud against the next-door neighbor's fence.

"*Gol-gol-gol-gol-gol-gol-gol-gol-gol-gol!*" he roared, imitating one of the football commentators on the radio, and he danced round the room with his eyes on the ceiling and his arms lifted heavenwards, the middle fingers of each hand tucked into the palm.

"I was going to eat that," I murmured.

Still. The things he could do.

As I began to put together a fresh pitcher of caipirinhas, there came a faint banging from overhead. Ronnie froze.

"It's only Maite," I told him. "She's got this broomstick. I think she might be a witch."

"Oh, now I get it," Ronnie said.

"Get what?"

"Why Cristiani's so upset with you."

"What are you on about?"

Ronnie gave me a knowing look. "Maite the witch."

"You've got the wrong end of the stick," I said. "You really have."

"What stick's that? A broomstick?"

I laughed, then tasted my new drink. "I make a pretty good caipirinha, if I say so myself."

"No flies on you, Nacho."

"Can I play something for you? Would you like that?"

As he followed me across the hallway, I could feel the buzz of the *cachaça* coming off him like a voltage, but he was nodding.

"It's a piece I've been working on," I told him. "Something Earl Hines used to play."

Ronnie paused on the threshold to the lounge and leaned one shoulder against the wall.

"Make yourself comfortable," I said.

"I'm fine here."

"You're going to slip out in the middle, aren't you. Like last time."

Ronnie's grin lacked its usual certainty.

"You leave whenever you want," I went on. "I won't be offended. Just don't try and cook, okay?"

I sat down in front of my Yamaha and switched it on, then I lowered my hands onto the keyboard, lightly as two butterflies landing on a flower.

THE FIRST MESSAGE came on a Sunday at the end of August 2008. Ronnie had been gone for a couple of months, and I'd had no contact with him at all. Every now and then, I would make the trip up to the house where he used to live. Sometimes I heard music, sometimes just the hiss of a lawn sprinkler. Once, the electronic gate slid open, and a Jaguar with tinted windows eased out into the street. It was so shiny I could see myself in it. I wondered who'd moved in. A local politician, maybe—or a member of the Bulgarian mafia. They were everywhere these days.

That Sunday, Ronnie was making his debut for AC Milan. His first touch was nothing special—a simple layoff to Clarence Seedorf—but the TV cameras were alive to the presence of the club's new signing, and they zoomed in on his face. That was when he winked at me. I'm serious. Ronnie could do things like that. You might be in a completely different world, but he could still communicate with you. It was the psychic equivalent of lobbing the ball over an advancing defender. A kind of *sombrero mental*. Only a few days earlier, I had watched a rerun of FC Barcelona's thumping of Real Madrid at the Bernabeu in November 2005. As Ronnie scored his first goal—Barça's second—I was struck by the way he seemed to vibrate or shimmer as he ran, as if electricity was flowing through his veins instead of blood. And then there was the sheer speed at which he moved. He appeared for those ten or fifteen seconds to have shifted into overdrive. But you had to be operating at a level close to his for the effect to register. If players like Sergio Ramos and Casillas were humiliated that night, it was because they were *good enough* to be humiliated. After Ronnie scored his second goal, in the seventy-seventh minute of the game, the massed ranks of supporters in the Bernabeu rose to their feet in their white shirts and applauded. This was unheard of, and their faces were grave, almost ashen. They couldn't hide their admiration, though. They had witnessed something that could never be repeated. They had a sense of how fleeting greatness is, and a sense too, I think, of the sweet brevity of life. Not just Ronnie's. Their own as well.

I had watched the match in a bar, with Ari, and I remember him explaining how injuries affect a footballer. They hurt him more than they would hurt you or me, he said in the patient, earnest voice he'd had as a young boy. There's the pain of the injury itself, and then there's another, far more agonizing pain—the pain of knowing that you're missing the moment. After all, you don't know how many moments you will have. As I watched the game again, three years later, I thought of Ronnie and his melancholic tendencies. His was an archetypal story—a unique and mercurial talent, a meteoric rise from rags to riches—but in the end he was a footballer, and he could only play for a limited amount of time. His powers would fade. Then what? A kind of afterlife—all the glory left behind, beyond retrieving. I thought of the gifted English player, Gascoigne, who almost drank himself to death in China towards the end of his career. How long would Ronnie be able to keep going? Though he was only twenty-five when he scored those goals at the Bernabeu, he had appeared to be at the top of his game. Would he ever be that good again?

The only time I touched on the subject was on his terrace one evening, the shadows lengthening across the pool.

"Do you think about what happens after this," I said, "when you're no longer playing?"

He gave me what I called his free-kick look—calculating and steady, from beneath his eyebrows. "Do you think about dying?"

I didn't answer. I simply held his gaze.

"It's the same question," he said. "I don't think about not playing. I just play."

I PROP MYSELF ON MY ELBOWS and look around. I still have no idea whose trousers I'm wearing, but the night is warm and the lawn feels soft and away to my left, oddly enough, is a white football that seems to glow in the darkness, as if lit from the inside.

One of these days, I expect to see Ronnie again.

He'll almost certainly surprise me, pulling up next to me in some top-of-the-range SUV. Diamond ear studs, black bandana. Bass notes pumping through the open window, loud enough to shake the neighborhood.

Or else I'll find him stretched out on my sofa, one arm draped over his eyes.

If he shows up when I'm not home, he always does the same thing. He rings the bell and waits a few moments, then he lets himself in.

After all, he still has a key.

THE CARPENTER OF MONTJUÏC

THE FIRST TIME I SAW Vic Drago, he was on his own. I was waiting at the bus stop outside my building when the glass front door swung open and a stocky man with thinning black hair emerged. He was wearing a maroon jacket, a black shirt, and black trousers with sharp creases. A gold chain bracelet glinted on his left wrist. He stopped to light a cigarette, then strode off along the street, smoke flowing over his shoulder as he exhaled.

I saw him again the following week, in the evening. This time he passed me on the pavement. He was with a heavy middle-aged woman who was carrying two Caprabo bags loaded with groceries, and he walked in front of her, his eyes on his phone, a newspaper tucked under one arm. Something about the way they talked to each other without looking at each other told me they were married. His choice of wife surprised me. I would have expected him to be with someone younger, more glamorous.

Two weeks later, the lift door opened one morning and he was facing me, his back to the fake teak paneling.

"Going down?" I said.

He nodded and yawned, both at the same time.

I stepped inside. The lift was small, with barely enough room for two people, and once the door was shut I was so close to him that we were almost touching. He smelled of cigarettes and aftershave. Something acrid, lemony.

"You speak English?" he said in *castellano.*

"Yes," I said.

He switched languages. "Do you live in the building?"

"I'm on the third floor, at the front."

"I've got the penthouse. *Sobreatico.*" He ran a hand over his hair, the gold chain bracelet shifting lazily on his wrist. "What a night."

"Were you out late?"

"I haven't been to bed yet."

I raised my eyebrows and nodded, as people do when they're impressed. After all, he wasn't a young man. Mid-forties, I would have said.

The lift jolted to a halt, then swayed a little on its cables. The door slid open. We crossed the lobby with its beige leatherette sofa and its plants rooted in beds of gray pebbles.

Outside, on the pavement, he asked if I would join him for a coffee. I glanced at my watch. I had a meeting in Sarrià at ten.

"It's all right," he said. "I won't keep you long."

I felt ungracious then.

We went to a bar round the corner, on Plaça Kennedy, where he ordered a *carajillo*. I had my usual *café con leche*. It was a cool, sunny morning, and we sat outside. I asked him how long he had lived in Barcelona. Three years, he said. Before that, he lived in London. Did I know London? I had studied there, I told him. In the mid-nineties. He hadn't wasted time with college, he said. He couldn't wait to get out in the real world. Start making money. These days, he owned three warehouses in North London, not far from the M1. I asked what the warehouses were used for. Storing documents, he said. It was lucrative, and the business pretty much ran itself. That was why he'd decided on a change of scene. I mean, why live in London if you don't have to? He spent an hour online every morning, then made a few phone calls. That was his working day.

"Sounds like you've got your life under control," I said.

He smiled complacently, then adjusted his gold bracelet. "What about you?"

"I translate books. Fiction, mostly."

He asked if the work was well paid. I told him what I earned—between three and five thousand euros per book. He was curious to know how long it took to translate a book. Three months, I said. Sometimes longer.

"Jesus," he said. "And you can live on that?"

I smiled. "I get by."

We both quietly sipped our coffees.

Before I left, he asked me up to his apartment the following week. He was having some friends over for drinks. Most of them were Catalan, like me.

"Any time after ten," he said. "Bring your girlfriend if you like."

"How do you know I have a girlfriend?"

"Obvious, isn't it—nice-looking bloke like you."

Was it the fifteen-year gap in our ages that allowed him to compliment me without the slightest awkwardness, or was it because we came from different countries, different cultures? I wasn't sure. Whatever the truth was, he was able to achieve an instant familiarity, and without having done anything to earn it.

I asked what his name was.

"Vic," he said. "Like the city."

He took out a business card and handed it to me. VIC DRAGO & PARTNERS. STORAGE SOLUTIONS.

"I'm Jordi," I said. "Jordi Ferrer."

He smiled with his mouth, but not, I noticed, with his eyes. "Translator. No wonder your English is so good."

THE FOLLOWING SATURDAY, I arranged to meet Mireia in a bar not far from her apartment. Mireia was the manager of the Dalí, a boutique hotel in the Eixample. I had known her since my schooldays, and in the summer of 1998, when we were in our early twenties, we had slept together, but she put an end to it after a couple of weeks. It doesn't feel right, she told me. We're supposed to be friends, not lovers. Can't we be both? I remember saying, and she let out a sigh, as if there was some basic principle I had failed to understand.

Though my mother knew and liked Mireia's family—my father and Mireia's father had worked at the same law firm—she had disapproved of our involvement from the beginning. She's not for you, she would say. She won't make you happy. I thought she was wrong, of course.

When I walked into the bar on Santaló, Mireia was already there, dressed in jeans close-fitting enough to show off her slim thighs and a zip-up leather jacket that was the same color as her hair, a kind of tawny brown. She had the face of an elf, fine-boned and triangular, and a high fringe that drew attention to her smooth forehead and her wide eyes. As always, I wanted to hold her tight and feel the full length of her against me. Instead, we kissed on both cheeks.

"You're so late," she said. "I've been here for ages."

Years ago, I had decided that if all I could ever hope for was her friendship the only way I could hold on to my self-esteem and even, now and then, exert a little power, was to be unpredictable. Pathetic, perhaps, but I couldn't help myself. The trouble was, unpredictability didn't come naturally to me. I really had to work at it.

I ordered a *caña*.

"Jordi, I've got to tell you something." Mireia leaned over the table, beckoning me closer, as if she was about to impart a secret. "I keep finding keys."

"What sort of keys?"

"Other people's keys. Keys they've lost." She took out a packet of Nobel and lit one. "What do you think it means?"

Not sure how to respond, I didn't say anything. I reached for my beer instead.

"The first key I found was a dull gold color," she went on. "For a front door, probably. Next, I found a tiny silver key, like the ones that come with a padlock—or a suitcase. Then, yesterday, I was in Sant Cugat, and I found these." She rummaged in her bag, took out a key ring holding perhaps a dozen keys, and put them on the table between us, then she brought her cigarette up to her mouth. I had always loved watching Mireia smoke. Her lips seemed made for cigarettes.

"You're staring at me," she said.

My eyes dropped to the bunch of keys. "That's someone's entire life you've got there," I said, and shivered.

Mireia shivered too. Then we both laughed.

Later, as we wandered along the Passeig Maritím, she hooked her arm through mine. The evening sky stretched before us, flawless as a cinema screen, and the palm trees looked black against the dimly glowing sea. A girl in aviator sunglasses roller-bladed past. Mireia leaned her head against my shoulder and murmured, *Ah Jordi,* not out of love, I thought, or even affection, but because I was a conundrum she had been presented with, a riddle she had no answer to.

THAT SPRING, I had three translations on the go at the same time, but one book interested me far more than the others. *Giving* was a short novel by a first-time French writer. The narrator was Jeanne, a middle-aged woman who discovers that her husband, Marc, is having an affair. Marc's lover is a woman in her twenties called Sophie. Jeanne doesn't leave

Marc. She doesn't even confront him. Instead, she hires a detective to find out where Sophie lives, and where she works. Once she has Sophie's two addresses, she begins to send her presents. Flowers, chocolates—the kind of things lovers give each other. Though the presents arrive anonymously—no card, no note—Sophie naturally assumes they're from Marc. She can't believe how romantic he is—how romantic and how discreet, since he never refers to anything he has bought for her. Early one afternoon, when they have finished making love—they always meet at her apartment, at lunchtime—she breaks her silence and thanks him. He has no idea what she's talking about. *Presents? What presents?* She stares at him, bewildered. In that moment, it occurs to Marc that Sophie might have another admirer, even, perhaps, another lover, but before he can say anything she promises him that there is no one else. The speed with which she preempts his question suggests to him that she is lying, and that he's right to be suspicious, and he leaves her apartment abruptly, without saying another word. This is what Jeanne imagines, knowing Marc as she does, since the novel consists almost entirely of hunches and speculations, scenes she couldn't possibly have witnessed. All she knows for sure is what she is able to observe—namely, that Sophie takes the rest of the day off, and Marc is distracted and irritable when he comes home. She continues to shower Sophie with presents. A red rose here, a silver locket there. Sophie believes Marc is filled with regret about having stormed out, and that he's trying to buy his way back into her affections. These new presents are peace offerings. A few days go by, and they agree to meet—at lunchtime in her apartment, as usual. When Marc appears, he kisses her, then tells her that he wants to make something clear. The presents she has been receiving are not from him. He hasn't given her *anything at all*. She thinks he's lying. But why would he do that? Why would he lie? She's utterly confused. Is that what you want? Marc says, his voice acidic now. To be *given* things? But if it's not you, Sophie says, who is it? Unconvinced by her protestations, Marc accuses her of cheating on him—and cheating twice over: firstly, because she's sleeping with somebody else, a fact she let slip without meaning to, and secondly, because she's pretending not to know the presents are from this other man. Sophie is beginning to feel her head might explode. If I knew they were from another man, she says, why would I ask if it was you? She has a point, but Marc can't see it. He's blinkered by his jealousy, his lack of trust. And actually, coming from you, Sophie goes on, this is all a bit rich. After all, I'm not the one who's being deceitful. I'm not the one who's *married*. Marc storms out again. From that day on, the nature of the presents begins to change. A courier delivers a small square package to Sophie's apartment. When she opens it, hundreds of red ants swarm out, stinging her hands. She screams and drops the box on the floor, then runs to the kitchen and holds her hands under the cold tap for a long time. Shortly afterwards, a Manila envelope arrives. Inside is a blown-up photo of Sophie with her eyes poked out. A week later, a pig's heart is posted to her place of work. Jeanne wonders what effect these new "presents" are having. It seems likely that Sophie will hold Marc responsible, since he obviously has a grudge against her, and is seeking a kind of vengeance. It's in the act of giving that he expresses all his deepest feelings, even if they're negative or hostile. The unpleasantness escalates. In the space of three days, Sophie receives a live bullet and a dead bird. By now, she's a nervous wreck. She sends Marc a text, telling him that if he doesn't stop at once she will contact the police. That weekend, he shows up unexpectedly. Stop what? he says. I haven't done anything. She refuses to discuss it. She's too upset. When she asks him to return the keys to her apartment, he loses his temper and throws them out of the window. He's childish, she says. Malicious. He may even be unhinged. He's staring at her. Why had he never noticed how shrill she sounded? How spoiled?

Though I kept thinking about the novella, I was finding it a challenge to translate. The atmosphere and tone were difficult to capture, maybe because the narrator, Jeanne, was such an enigma. She revealed nothing about herself, except through the characters she interacted with—her husband, and his lover. Except by default. And there was something else. I couldn't rid myself of the feeling that the book was haunting me for a reason. It was as if it was commenting obliquely on my own personal situation. Perhaps it even included strategies that might prove useful. But they weren't obvious to me. They lurked beneath the surface of the narrative, like fish at the bottom of a pond. Though the book was set in Lyon, I pictured Mireia passing beneath Sophie's living-room window, picking the keys up off the pavement, and showing them to me later, in the bar on Santaló. My life and my work were echoing each other—but to what end?

Y
OU'RE THE FIRST TO ARRIVE," Vic said.

When I walked into his apartment at ten o'clock on Thursday evening, he gave me a beer from the fridge, then led me through his living room and out onto a terrace that was the size of a five-a-side football pitch. Though I lived in the same building, it felt like a different world. Most of the city was laid out before me, all the way from Horta in the north to the Zona Franca and the Mediterranean in the southwest. Rising in front of us were the hills of the Collserola, their dark, scrubby slopes studded with mansions, and crowned by the floodlit church on the top of Tibidabo. Vic went and leaned on the railing at the edge of the terrace, and I joined him.

"What do you think?" he said.

I shook my head. "Amazing."

"The moment I saw this view, I had to have the place."

"Did you buy it?"

"It's a rental." Vic lit a cigarette and blew smoke into the void. "You didn't bring your girlfriend."

"She's working tonight."

He looked at me askance, as if he suspected me of lying—and I was, though not quite in the way he imagined. I watched the planes coming in to land, bright drops of light that seemed to wobble as they slid down through the deep blue of the sky towards El Prat.

"Something strange," Vic said after a while.

It began in December last year, he went on. One afternoon, he was standing outside an estate agents' in Sarrià, looking at the prices of apartments, when a man in a long dark overcoat appeared next to him. The man asked if he knew Bill Stone. Vic looked at the man. Yes, I know Bill Stone, he said. Bill worked at the international school where his wife Joanna taught.

"You remind me of him somehow—though you're younger, of course." The man smiled.

Vic didn't get the joke. Bill Stone was pushing seventy, with almost no hair and a beer gut, and he, Vic, was only forty-four. He asked how the man knew Bill.

"I made him a rocking chair," the man said.

"A rocking chair?"

"I work with wood."

"Could you make me a chest of drawers?"

Vic had surprised himself. Though it was true that he and Joanna had agreed that the hallway needed a chest of drawers, he hadn't actually started looking for one, let alone thought of having one made. He had never even had a suit made. The words seemed to have been teased out of him. No, not teased. Extracted. Without his knowledge or permission. The man was eyeing him with an innocent, wondering expression, as if he was still marveling at Vic's resemblance to Bill Stone. He handed Vic a business card, which Vic studied in the light of a nearby streetlamp.

DANIEL FEDERMANN. There was an address too. Somewhere downtown. His eyes lifted to the man's face. "You don't look like someone who works with wood."

Though the man was no longer smiling, a residue of good humor remained. "I don't?"

"I would've taken you for a solicitor," Vic went on, "or even"—and he used a thumb to indicate the window behind him—"an estate agent."

The man nodded. He seemed to understand that Vic was getting his own back, and it didn't bother him. Perhaps he felt he'd asked for it.

"If you'd really like something made," he said, "come to my workshop, and we'll discuss it. I'm there most days."

He drew his overcoat more closely around himself, then turned away. Though Vic kept his eyes on the man, he had the impression that he simply dissolved into the air. One moment he was there, the next he was gone. But it was dusk by then, and a swirling mist had filled the narrow streets of Sarrià...

Still leaning on the railing, Vic drank some beer, then he looked at me. "I haven't told anyone about this. To be honest, I'm not sure why I'm telling you."

It was because I looked presentable, I thought. Unthreatening. I kept my hair cut short, though not overly short, and I wore glasses with simple frames, nothing too modern or pretentious. My clothes were pretty conservative as well. Jackets and jeans. Open-necked white shirts. Brown shoes. Or maybe he recognized a kind of attentiveness in me. I'd always been a good listener.

"What do you think so far?" Vic said. "What's your feeling?"

"It sounds like the beginning of a story."

"You mean, like I made it up?"

"No. It sounds as if it's going to lead to something."

"Oh, it does." Vic's jaw tightened. "It does."

The doorbell rang, and Vic went to answer it. A couple appeared. The man was roughly Vic's age, and wore a biker's leather jacket with a white nuclear disarmament symbol on the back. The girl was in her early twenties. Vic showed them where the drinks were and told them to make themselves at home, then he opened the fridge, grabbed two more bottles of beer, and came outside again.

"You went to see him, didn't you," I said. "The carpenter."

Vic laughed, then handed me a beer. "You're not as stupid as you look."

Shock or bemusement must have showed on my face because he slapped me on the shoulder. "Don't be so sensitive. It was a joke."

"A joke." I nodded to myself. "Okay."

Even at that stage, I saw how little use Vic had for diplomacy or tact. He didn't care if he upset people. I wondered how many enemies he had.

A few days after his encounter outside the estate agents', Vic said, he was driving down Las Ramblas when he decided to make a detour. He was curious to know where the carpenter's workshop was. He had no intention of having a chest of drawers made, though as he parked in a side street off Avinguda Parallel he felt a twist of anticipation low down in his belly, an excitement he couldn't explain.

Once he located the street, he walked from one end to the other, but he couldn't find a house number that corresponded to the one on the card the carpenter had given him. He walked back again, then stood still, staring. How could he have missed it? He set off again, moving more slowly. The street divided straight down the middle, half sunlight, half shade. At the far end, it formed a T-junction with an unpaved track that hugged the steep, rocky flank of Montjuïc. In the distance he could hear the howl of a chainsaw.

He would never have found the place if he hadn't glanced to his right as he was returning to his car. There, framed by an open ground-floor window that was covered with a rusting metal grille, was the carpenter. He was sitting down, head bent, as if reading or writing. Vic approached the door and tapped on one of the glass panes, which rattled in its frame. The door opened, and Federmann appeared. Vic didn't have to remind him of the chance meeting in Sarrià a few nights earlier. Federmann had not forgotten.

"I didn't expect you so soon," he said.

Vic shrugged. "I happened to be passing."

If Federmann knew Vic was lying, he didn't let on.

"Come in," he said. "Please."

The interior of the workshop was tidy, but it had not been renovated or modernized. An old-fashioned writing desk stood by the window, a leather-bound ledger open on its sloping surface.

Federmann took a bottle of red wine from the shelf behind him. "Can I offer you a drink?"

"I just thought I'd drop in and say hello," Vic said. "I'm not here to buy anything."

Federmann smiled.

Uncorking the bottle, he poured them both a glass. Vic had an odd thought, which came quite unsolicited, and which he didn't fully understand. *I'm not the first.*

They touched glasses. A thin, ringing note hung on in the air.

"Let me show you round," Federmann said.

The front of the workshop functioned as a showroom, with a number of pieces of furniture on display, but as Vic followed Federmann deeper into the place, passing beneath a skylight, the space opened out. There was a long worktable, fitted with various lathes and vises. Rows of tools lined the walls. But there were also objects that seemed far less predictable. A crossbow, a brass astrolabe—and half a dozen snakeskins, which hung from a wooden beam like strips of flypaper. They were so delicate that they stirred as Vic walked by.

Federmann came to a halt with his back to Vic, both hands in his pockets. Vic glanced over his shoulder. A fall of dusty light stood between him and the front of the shop, and he could no longer see the door. Though it was by no means warm, he realized he was sweating.

They had stopped in front of a chest of drawers that was so pale that it hardly appeared to have a color, and as soon as Vic set eyes on it he could see it in his hallway. He could see it so clearly that he felt he wasn't in the shadow of Montjuïc at all, or even downtown, but back in his apartment in Sant Gervasi.

"One of yours?" His voice came out husky, diminished.

Federmann nodded.

"It looks expensive," Vic said.

"It isn't cheap. But this is just a social visit, remember?"

All the same, he began to tell Vic about the piece. The wood was Russian birch, he said, imported from Siberia. The fact that it had been cut at night, by the light of a full moon, gave it an unusual responsiveness, a special pliancy. It explained the pallor too, perhaps. As a rule, Vic had no patience with this kind of superstitious nonsense, but the carpenter's voice had become hypnotic, and it was as if the skeptical side of Vic's nature had been bypassed or overridden. Before he knew it, he had reached out and placed a hand on the top of the chest of drawers. It felt smooth. Cool. It reminded him of something. Something he hadn't touched in a long time—or something he had only imagined touching. He looked up. Federmann was watching him with an expression he couldn't decipher.

Bending down, Vic examined the piece of furniture more closely. It had a slightly asymmetrical quality, its edges appearing to undulate. Knots showed in its stumpy legs. Though Vic hadn't spoken, Federmann seemed to read his mind. He had respected the wood's inherent character, he said. He had followed the grain. There were four drawers—two small ones at the top and two large ones underneath. The metal handles were the color of verdigris, and they had a rustic look. When Vic slid one of the large drawers open, it rumbled like distant thunder. The inside smelled of forests. Moss.

Siberia, Vic thought.

He paid for the chest of drawers by credit card and arranged to have it delivered. The transaction took no more than a few minutes. Once Federmann had entered Vic's details in his ledger, he turned away and consulted the calendar on the wall behind him. Vic surreptitiously scanned the previous entries. There was no sign of a Bill Stone.

When the delivery men set down the chest of drawers in the hallway three days later, Vic's wife Joanna gave him an odd look.

"This isn't like you," she said.

"To buy furniture?"

She shook her head. "To get it right."

He was about to take offense, but then he caught himself. If the truth be told, he was also surprised at himself—and he went on being surprised. He would find himself in cafés and bars, repeating Federmann's lines about Siberia, the full moon, and the wood's rare flexibility, not just to Joanna, but to friends as well, and no one took the piss or even questioned what he was saying. They reacted just as he'd reacted. They were riveted.

Vic turned to me, sweat gleaming on his forehead. "But you know what, Jordi? I couldn't help feeling there was something fishy going on."

"Fishy?"

"What he was doing," Vic went on, "it felt like a challenge. A threat."

I stared at him. "I don't understand."

Vic's face was sickly pale all of a sudden. "You're not the only one."

"Where is it now? I didn't notice it on the way in."

"It's right behind you."

Startled, I swung round. The chest of drawers stood at the back of the terrace, near the barbecue. I looked at Vic, as if for guidance or permission, but he gave me nothing. I crossed the terrace. As I approached, I felt a magnetic pull, not just the urge to reach out and touch the chest of drawers, but something palpable or physical, a kind of tug. It didn't come from me. It came from outside. *From the thing itself.* I didn't touch it, though. I stepped back instead.

"Why is it outdoors?" I said. "What if it rains?"

But Vic didn't seem to be listening. "The full moon. Siberia—" He let out a disdainful, almost bitter laugh. "I mean, it's crazy, right?"

I saw that he needed something from me—corroboration, or reassurance. "I don't know what to say. I'm sorry. I'm not being much use."

He stared off into the hills again, and for a few seconds I sensed his thoughts, as dark and tangled as the woodlands of the Collserola.

"What does your wife think?" I asked.

He shrugged. "She likes it."

I looked around. "Where is she, anyway?"

"Sleeping."

A voice called from the living room. More people had arrived. He said we'd better go in.

"What I told you," he added. "Keep it to yourself."

Vic's guests had settled round the glass-topped coffee table, rolling spliffs and chopping white powder into lines. Vic made caipirinhas in a big jug. He told me he had learned the recipe from a friend in the restaurant business in Castelldefels. Within half an hour the apartment was packed. Vic put on the latest Amy Winehouse record—he owned a large collection of vinyl—and people started dancing.

We didn't get the chance to talk again.

ON FRIDAY NIGHT a storm rolled in, violent and yet incomplete, with sheet lightning and bursts of thunder, but no real rain. I stood at my living-room window, staring down into Avinguda de la República Argentina. The 22 bus roared past. Bleary greenish-yellow windows, hardly anyone inside. It was March, and people would have left for the mountains. There was still some snow up there.

Earlier that day, Montse had called. She was publishing the French novella I was working on. Married to Jaume, one of my literature professors at university, she was a glamorous, chain-smoking woman in her late forties. She wanted to know how the translation was going, and I told her progress was slow. I was having trouble capturing the tone of voice. It was so brilliantly airless and corrosive.

"Take your time, love," Montse said. "It's got to be good."

Corrosive. Was that the word? Though Jeanne narrated the story, she remained underwritten and uninhabited throughout. At first, I admired her bravado—her unconventional approach to what was essentially a conventional predicament—but as the book evolved, her behavior became disproportionate, and I began to wonder what kind of monster I was listening to. When did being in the right turn into being in the wrong? At what point did the victim become the perpetrator? To what extent was Jeanne actually enjoying the bewilderment and terror of her rival, Sophie? And where, in the end, did the reader's sympathies lie? These were the questions the novella raised. But the title—*Giving*—which was obvious and flat, offered no easy answers. Perhaps what the book was really about was not infidelity and revenge but the way in which we're altered by pressures we're not accustomed to. There was even the implication that Jeanne had been waiting for a situation like this to arise. Part of her had been lying dormant—hoping…

A vicious flash of silver. For a split second, the people on the pavement below had shadows, even though it was after eleven o'clock at night. I walked over to my desk and shut down my computer. Once, during a storm, there had been a power surge, and I had lost an entire week's work. I found myself thinking of Mireia. She lived on her own, and storms frightened her. As I called her mobile, the thunder came, long-drawn-out and ponderous, like a bowling ball sent rolling down its lane. The moment before the skittles scatter.

"God, did you hear that?" Her voice was trembling.

To distract her, I began to tell her about the carpenter's workshop at the foot of Montjuïc, and the chest of drawers made from wood that had been cut by the light of a full moon.

"You're making this up," she said.

"I'm not. It's true." But I tried to sound as if I was lying. I wanted to take some credit for the story. Anything to impress her—even now, after all these years.

"So what happened?"

"A man came across the workshop by chance. He just walked in and looked around, all very casual. When he saw the chest of drawers, though, he fell in love with it. Instantly. It reminded him of something—he couldn't think what—but he knew one thing: he had to have it."

Mireia laughed softly. "I'm a bit like that."

"I know."

A crack of thunder, then a nasty tearing sound, as if bits of canvas were being ripped to pieces in the sky.

Mireia gasped.

I asked if she was all right.

"Keep talking," she said.

I remembered the night we went for a walk in the Collserola. It was Mireia's idea. After dinner, we drove up Muntaner and through the tunnels, leaving the *carretera* at Valldoreix. We parked on a suburban road and set off along the dirt track that leads to Can Borell, a restaurant deep in the woods. It was July, and the moon was almost full. The track was dusty, pale as flour. I could see Mireia's face quite clearly.

Once we had passed the huge two-hundred-year-old pine tree known as El Pi d'en Xandri, the track narrowed. Only a few hundred meters farther on, Mireia suggested we take a smaller path, one she seemed to choose at random. I was worried about wild boar—I had heard of people being attacked—and also about getting lost, but I decided to say nothing. Still, there was a ribbon of fear in me as I plunged after her, into the bushes. The path wound upwards, over rocks and roots. We were following a dried-up watercourse. If we came in winter, we would be walking in a stream. After a quarter of an hour we reached the summit of a low hill. The undergrowth was taller than we were. There was no view. It was here, just to one side of the path, that we found a small clearing with a floor of pine needles, a kind of chamber in the forest. Now we were standing still, I realized we were both breathing hard from the climb.

"It's like a little room," Mireia said in a hushed voice.

We would never be more hidden, I thought, or more alone.

She kneeled down.

"The ground's still warm," she said. "Feel."

She was looking up at me, lips parted. The sight of her drew all the air out of me. I felt my heart was beating in a vacuum.

"Jordi?" she murmured.

I kneeled.

For once I managed not to tell her what she meant to me. That always ruined everything. Instead I talked about the beauty of the night, the wildness of where we were. The sense that we could be the only people in the world. A soft sound came out of her. Half sigh, half groan. As if I'd hurt her. We took off our clothes and made love on the pine needles, her body monochrome but edged in silver as it rose above me, and I whispered to myself, Remember this, remember everything. There will come a time when you won't believe it happened.

"Jordi?"

Ah yes. The storm, the story...

"The man bought the chest of drawers," I said, resuming, "and had it delivered to his apartment. A few hours later, when he woke up in the middle of the night, he saw the chest of drawers standing across the room, next to the door. It was giving off a strange kind of muted light, like an aura, and it was then that he realized what it reminded him of—"

Mireia interrupted. "What? What did it remind him of?"

"It reminded him of a girl he used to know—how her skin looked in the dark when they made love..."

I could hear Mireia on the other end, holding her breath. She was only millimeters away from me, it seemed. I wondered if she understood the reference. I doubted it somehow. It was possible she no longer remembered the night that I could not forget.

Still, I went on.

"He walked over and touched the wood, and it was as soft as her skin, and he knew then that he would have paid anything for that chest of drawers. Because the girl it reminded him of was a girl who had been killed in a car crash several years before. She'd been on holiday in France, and she was driving back to Barcelona to be with him. She missed him so much that she was driving fast—too fast—and that was when she lost control—"

I stopped, partly out of shock—until that moment I hadn't realized that the girl might be dead—and partly because I wasn't sure where I could take the story next.

"Is that the end?" Mireia asked.

"I don't know. Maybe she shouldn't have died. Maybe something else should have happened—something less dramatic, but just as tragic."

"I think the storm's moved on."

"Yes."

"You know what, Jordi? You should write."

"I haven't got anything to say. That's why I do translations."

She sighed. I had disappointed her.

"It's late," I said. "I should get some sleep."

"Thank you so much for calling."

Something hot surged through me, like a car accelerating from a standing start. "Mireia—"

But she'd already gone.

I BECAME A REGULAR at the café on Plaça Kennedy where Vic had taken me on the day we first met. Most mornings, I would order *café con leche* and a croissant, then I would go back to my apartment and start work. Though Vic and I kept different hours, I knew I would run into him sooner or later.

During the first week of May I walked in to find him sitting by the window in a pink bowling shirt, reading a copy of *Mundo Deportivo*. The paper was open on a photo of Ronaldinho, his face tipped skywards, the two middle fingers of each hand tucked into the palm. Though football didn't interest me much, I knew this was how the Brazilian celebrated when he scored a goal. Vic looked up. He hadn't shaved, and his eyes were bloodshot.

"Can I join you?" I asked.

"Be my guest." He didn't seem especially glad to see me, and I wondered if I'd done something to offend him.

I ordered my usual *café con leche*.

He asked if I'd seen the game on Sunday. I shook my head. He told me it had been a shambles.

"Shambles," I said. "Such a great word." I gestured at the picture of Ronaldinho. "Is it true he's leaving?"

Vic shrugged. "That's what they say."

"Are you all right, Vic? You look tired."

"I just got back from London. I have to show up now and then—keep the bastards on their toes." He pushed the paper away and lit a cigarette. "Do you believe in the supernatural?"

"You mean, like ghosts?" I was smiling.

"I'm serious." He turned his cigarette in the ashtray until the tip was sharp and red. "Have you had any experiences you couldn't explain?"

"Like what?"

"Noises in the night—stuff moving about—"

I assumed a pensive look, but I wasn't actually thinking about anything at all. In that moment, I felt like I was in a movie. Vic often had that effect on me.

"I'm not sure," I said. "What are you getting at?"

He rolled his shoulders inside his shirt, then crushed out his cigarette and shook his wrist, adjusting the position of his gold chain bracelet. "Are you free tomorrow night?"

I said I was.

He asked if I knew a bar called the Mirador. It was at the top of Avinguda Tibidabo. I thought I'd seen a bar up there, but I'd never been to it.

"Meet me there at eleven," he said.

Seconds later, he had me staring at him open-mouthed as he told me a story that involved, among other things, two male strippers from Venezuela performing in a derelict ballroom in Les Corts.

I ARRIVED EARLY the following night. Taking a seat at the bar, I ordered a beer and looked around. I could see why Vic might frequent the Mirador. With its seventies wood paneling, its red banquettes, and its small square dance floor, it had a seedy *Saturday Night Fever* feel to it, and the front wall was a single plate-glass window that overlooked the whole of Barcelona. Vic liked a view. I wondered where Mireia was. I wondered who she was with. The jealousy was dull, like a headache only partially suppressed by painkillers. Far below, the lights of the city winked and glittered, as if they were in on the secret.

I was already on my second beer when Vic showed up. He was dressed in a mustard-yellow jacket with a black polo neck and his usual pressed black trousers. He ordered a rum-and-Coke. When the drink arrived, he stared down into the glass, stabbing at the ice cubes with a plastic cocktail stick. The signet ring he was wearing gave off a sullen gleam.

"You asked me why I kept the chest of drawers outside," he said.

I nodded. "I was curious."

"It started about a month ago."

He had got home late, he went on, and he had gone straight to bed. At four a.m., he was woken by a scraping noise that seemed to be coming from inside the apartment. At first he thought it was Joanna—chronic back pain often disturbed her during the night—but she was fast asleep beside him. He lay motionless, just listening. There were no more noises. In the morning he found a note from Joanna on the breakfast bar. *Could you be a bit quieter when you come in?*

Some of us have to get up in the morning. He had no idea what she was on about.

A week later, she accused him of having moved the chest of drawers into the living room. He could at least have moved it back again afterwards, she said, instead of leaving her to do it, with her slipped disc.

He was indignant. "I didn't move it. Why would I do that?"

"Maybe you don't *remember* moving it."

"It wasn't me."

She turned away, as if to protect herself. "You were probably out of it—as usual."

They'd had a fierce argument—it didn't take much these days—but the mystery remained unsolved.

Vic brushed the tip of his nose with the back of his hand, then glanced around. The Mirador had filled up while he'd been talking. Farther along the bar was a middle-aged man in a blazer. With his dyed blond mullet and his perma-tan he looked like an aging tennis star. The girl with him was wearing six-inch heels and lots of gold.

"Another drink?" I said.

Vic pushed his empty glass towards me. "Cheers."

A fresh rum-and-Coke in front of him, Vic picked up where he had left off. The next time he heard noises, he was alone in the apartment. Joanna was in England, seeing family. Again he lay still and listened. A kind of tapping. A scuffling too. He eased out of bed and moved to the door, which he always left half-open. Had someone broken in? Fists clenched, he edged down the corridor and then turned right, into the hall. The chest of drawers was gone. How could that be? He checked the front door. It was locked. The tapping and scuffling sounded closer now. He crept towards the living room, then stopped again, hardly daring to breathe. The noises had stopped as well. The sliding glass door at the far end of the living room was open. From where he stood, he could see pinpoints of light flashing on the famous communications tower in the hills. He could have sworn he'd closed the door before he went to bed.

He moved slowly across the room, keeping to the wall opposite the fireplace, where the shadows were deeper. Once he reached the door, he peered through the gap. The terrace looked the same as always. Could the intruder have escaped over the roof? Was that even *possible*? Or maybe it wasn't an intruder at all. Maybe the tapping and scuffling had come from a neighboring apartment. But in that case where was the chest of drawers? And why was the door open?

A gentle breeze stirred the plants Joanna had brought back from the garden center in Pedralbes. He slid the door shut and locked it, then he faced into the room, his head lowered, one hand wrapped round the back of his neck.

He was halfway to the kitchen, thinking he would make himself a drink, when there was a sudden crash behind him. It was so loud and so close to him that he cried out. He swung around, then froze. A fully grown wild boar stood on the terrace, only ten or fifteen feet away. The boar was glaring at him through the door, its breath clouding the glass. Its two short tusks curved viciously. Its eyes were small and fierce. He stepped backed, towards the kitchen, then he froze again. It had occurred to him that if he moved he might antagonize the creature. As he was wondering what to do next, the boar trotted over to the railing at the far edge of the terrace. Then it turned and charged. Its tusks struck the door with such force that the plate glass seemed to bulge inwards.

"Christ!"

The glass held firm, and the boar stood there as before, its eyes fixed on him, knowing and unkind. How could he protect himself? His thoughts struggled to emerge. He remembered a gun he had owned once, in London. He could see it in his hand—the blunt muzzle, the steely half-moon of the trigger. Stepping forwards quickly, he shoved the sofa lengthways against the door. The boar still hadn't moved. Its bristly flanks were heaving, as if it had exerted itself. He backed across the room, then turned and hurried down the passageway into his bedroom and shut the door behind him. He had never noticed how flimsy it was, no more than an inch thick. Wedging himself into the gap between the wardrobe and the wall, he pushed the wardrobe sideways until it covered the door, then he climbed into bed. He was sweating. His watch said ten past three.

He lay in the dark and thought about the wild boar. He thought about the surprisingly delicate tapping of its hooves on the tiled terrace. He thought about its rank breath on the glass. He thought about its eyes. The wind rose. An awning had come loose somewhere nearby. He could hear it fluttering and flapping.

The sweat cooled on his forehead, and on his throat.

Vic gulped savagely at his rum-and-Coke. "I kept thinking it must have been a dream. But the wardrobe was in front of the door when I woke up." He picked up his cocktail stick and studied it. "I'm telling you all this because you're the most down-to-earth person I know."

Down-to-earth? I wasn't so sure that was a compliment.

"What happened the next day?" I asked.

"The sofa was by the window, where I'd left it, but there was no sign of the wild boar."

"And the chest of drawers?"

"It was on the terrace, lying on its side."

"How did it get there?"

"I've no idea."

He seemed impatient suddenly. Did he think I wasn't taking him seriously enough, or had he been hoping I would be the voice of reason? *A wild boar on your terrace? That's crazy, Vic. You're nine floors up.* But he had told the story so vividly—so persuasively—that I'd found myself believing it.

Three women came in. Long hair, short skirts. Their slim tanned fingers juggled cigarettes and phones.

Vic knocked back his drink. "Let's go somewhere else."

Outside, the air was warm and still. A few long clouds were stacked in the sky above Montjuïc, their edges scalloped, silvery. Vic took out a key fob and unlocked a sleek black Lexus. I nodded to myself. It was just the kind of car I'd imagined he would have.

As we drove back down the hill, a Phil Collins CD on the sound system, Vic asked how my girlfriend was.

I smiled. "You mean, the girlfriend you've never seen?"

He looked across at me. "I've seen her."

"When?"

"A week or two ago, in the Eixample. You were with her."

He guided his Lexus down a slip road and onto the Ronda General Mitre. I wondered where we were going. The derelict ballroom in Les Corts?

"I hit the horn," he said, "but you didn't hear me."

Perhaps because he had confided in me, I began to tell him about Mireia. I had loved her for years, I said, even though we hadn't slept together more than a handful of times. I would do anything for her. But she thought of me as a friend, and she saw other men.

"Sounds like she needs a good slap," Vic said.

I looked at him. He wasn't joking. I remembered his wife carrying all the plastic bags from Caprabo, and him strolling in front of her, studying his phone.

"What?" He had felt my shocked gaze.

"You don't know her."

He glanced at me, his eyes oddly sure and blank. "You've got to show them who's boss or they walk all over you."

I laughed, but more out of nervousness than anything else. "That wouldn't work with Mireia."

"Oh no?"

I kept silent.

As we approached Sant Antoni market, Vic turned onto a dark street and parked.

"Mireia," he said quietly.

TWO DAYS LATER, on Saturday, I woke earlier than usual. I stood at the window in my bare feet, with coffee brewing in the kitchenette behind me and *No es un día cualquiera* on the radio, the sound down low. The hills at the back of the city looked veiled. Even the palm trees in the middle of Plaça d'Alfonso Comín lacked definition, their branches blurred by the milky air. These humid, almost tropical mornings always reminded me of Southeast Asia. I had flown to Bali once to try and forget about Mireia, but as I sat gazing out over the curving rice terraces near Ubud I had missed her more than I thought possible. Like a photo without a subject, the landscape only drew attention to her absence, and I felt more aware of her and more alone than I would have done if I had stayed in Barcelona. It was the worst holiday ever.

The coffee was ready. I poured myself a cup and carried it over to my laptop, where page 91 of *Giving* was waiting for me. On Thursday night, after drinks at the Mirador, Vic had taken me to a party in a converted warehouse. He pressed the buzzer next to a metal door, and when the intercom crackled into life he put his mouth close to the speaker.

"Lluis? Sóc jo. Vic."

"Ja ho sabia. Que vols?" The teasing voice was half submerged in talking and music.

"Obre la porta, cabró."

There was a laugh, then the door clicked open, and we took a cagelike lift to the fifth floor.

"Have you been working on your Catalan?" I asked.

Vic rolled his shoulders under his yellow jacket. "I know a few words."

The lift came to a halt.

"This should be interesting," he said.

We walked through double doors into a loft space that had rough brick walls, a polished concrete floor, and metal pillars. Tall windows at the far end looked towards Avinguda Parallel and Montjuïc. The glass kept changing color as a neon sign on the street outside shifted between blue and pink. There was a kitchen area in one corner. A short man with a shaved head was cooking squid.

"That's our host, Lluis," Vic said. "He's a DJ."

I felt out of place in my blue-and-white-striped shirt and my chinos, and wasn't sure why I'd agreed to come. Not that Vic had given me much choice. A thin black-haired girl in a red sleeveless top asked if I had any coke on me. When I said no, she began to talk about São Paulo, where she'd just spent a year. Did I know São Paulo? I shook my head. She'd had a Brazilian boyfriend, she told me. He was a video artist. Really talented. They'd had an amazing life. She went on and on about São Paulo, and it wasn't long before I was thoroughly sick of the place, even though I'd never been there. At one point, as I was listening, I closed my eyes, and when I opened them again, the girl was still talking. She didn't seem to have noticed—or perhaps she thought I was trying to picture her "amazing life." I'd been holding my empty glass for so long that it felt like part of my hand.

"If it was all so great," I said, "why did you leave?"

She didn't answer. She was too busy telling me how her video artist lover had chartered a private jet with some hedge-fund friends, and how they'd all taken MDMA and flown up to Rio for a night of clubbing.

Vic appeared and said he needed a favor.

"Anything," I said.

To my relief, he guided me away from the São Paulo girl and into a corner.

"Next time you're downtown," he said, "I want you to go and see Federmann."

"The carpenter?"

"Just wander into his workshop. Talk to him a bit." Vic lit a cigarette and let the smoke trickle from his nose. "You know about people, right? All that translating you do. I want to know what you think."

I watched Vic with what I hoped was an inscrutable expression—the kind of expression that someone who knew about people might adopt.

"He won't suspect anything," Vic went on. "I mean, look at you. You're so straight."

"Thanks, Vic."

"The way you dress—your hair, your glasses..."

"You make it sound like I'm in disguise."

Vic laughed.

But suddenly the idea of playing a cameo role in one of his bizarre scenarios appealed to me.

"All right," I said. "I'll do it."

Vic gripped my shoulder, his eyes intense and dark. "I owe you one."

I stared at my computer screen. The document I was working on had been left untouched for so long that the screensaver had clicked on. Colors whirled and flared through a blackness that was like deep space. I stood up, went over to the kitchenette, and poured myself another coffee.

What had I let myself in for?

THAT AFTERNOON, when I finished work, I took the metro to Drassanes. In ten minutes I was standing on the street Vic had described. I walked to the far end, where a stone wall marked the edge of Montjuïc, the ground rising steeply, the dry earth sprouting weeds. There were a few parked cars, no people. Areas like this were common in Barcelona, buildings giving way to wastelands of colorless grass and pale dust. But it didn't feel like the kind of place you came across by chance. It wasn't on the way to anywhere. Would Daniel Federmann see through me? My heart was beating high up in my throat.

I walked back to where the workshop was. The window was open. I put my head close to the metal grille and peered through. I could see the writing desk Vic had mentioned, and the wooden furniture beyond, ghostly in the gloom, but there was no sign of the carpenter.

"Can I help you?"

I jumped.

Federmann was standing to my left, in the doorway. How was it that I hadn't noticed him?

"Are you open?" I said.

"Yes, I'm open."

He was in his early forties, with smooth skin and wavy black hair that was beginning to go gray. I thought there was something indeterminate or evasive about his good looks. If the police had asked me to create a Photofit, I would've found it difficult.

"Do you mind if I look around?"

He didn't answer the question. He simply stood to one side and let me through, then followed me into the shop.

"How did you hear about me?" The question was casual, but his gaze was intense and focused, like a thumb on a pressure point.

"I didn't. I just happened to be passing." I hesitated, then had a flash of inspiration. "I've always liked old places. Places that seem—I don't know—hidden..."

I turned my back on him and moved slowly past a row of chairs and tables, pretending to admire the craftsmanship. Had I said too much? I reached the skylight Vic had mentioned. The pane of glass was cracked and smeared, the blue sky barely visible beyond. But I shouldn't be thinking of Vic, I told myself. I shouldn't even let his name enter my head. *I just happened to be passing, and I was curious. Thought I'd take a look around.* I forced myself to come up with a question.

"Did you make all this furniture yourself?"

"Some," he said. "Not all."

His eyes were on me again, calm and yet insistent. I moved deeper into the workshop. The walls were naked brick, and the air had a motionless, grainy quality that felt ancient. Like the inside of a pyramid. Like a tomb. It was only a matter of time before he realized what I was up to. Don't do anything, Vic had said. Just talk to him. I glanced towards the front of the shop and felt something of the panic Vic had felt. I wasn't sure I'd be able to make it to the door. As for the sunlit street, that seemed quite unattainable. Federmann was on his feet, still watching me. His gaze stretched between us across the dark interior like a beam of light or a length of silver wire.

"There's really nothing I can help you with?"

I hurried back through the workshop, almost knocking a chair over. My legs felt unreliable. I brushed past Federmann without looking at him, and yet I was aware of his face close up, and had the sense that it had altered, become the face of someone else, someone less benign.

"Sorry," I said. "An appointment. I have to go."

Once outside, I broke into a run.

On Avinguda Parallel, a dark-skinned man leaned against a third-floor balcony, smoking. He wore a pair of trousers—nothing else. He had a word tattooed across his chest. From where I stood, I couldn't make out what it said. A parrot tore through the air above me. A blur of green, a single high-pitched screech. I wiped the sweat off my forehead, then sat down on a bench and watched the traffic.

On Monday morning I met Vic in the café on Plaça Kennedy. He had ordered his usual *carajillo*. The moment I sat down, he asked if I'd managed to see Federmann.

"Yes, I saw him," I said.

Vic's whole body tensed. "What did you think?"

My first instinct, oddly, was not to divulge any information at all. It was as if I had unwittingly entered into a pact with the carpenter. Could Federmann still see me, even though I was on the other side of the city? Was he exerting some kind of influence?

"Well?"

I sipped my coffee and when I had replaced the cup on the saucer the feeling was gone. I began to try and describe my visit to the workshop. "There's something—I don't know..."

Vic leaned forwards, over the table, and grabbed my wrist. "Come on, Jordi. Spit it out."

"Something—*suspicious.*"

"Right." Vic let go of my wrist and sat back in his chair.

I hadn't really meant to say "suspicious." I'd been looking for a word that was subtler, and more suggestive, but he had rushed me. Who was the real adversary here? And why was I even thinking in those terms? Vic finished his coffee, then looked out of the window. He seemed satisfied—temporarily, at least.

I left the café not long afterwards. As I approached my apartment, Montse called. I assumed she wanted an update on my progress with the novella, but she had something else on her mind.

"Jordi," she said, "did I ever tell you about my ex?"

"Yes, you did." I remembered a story about an alcoholic jazz musician who lived down the coast.

"He rang me the other night. Told me he'd been giving Ronaldinho Spanish lessons—"

I couldn't help laughing.

"You think it isn't true?"

"If Ronaldinho wanted Spanish lessons," I said, "Barça would have organized them for him."

"That's what I thought." She paused. "He was pretty drunk."

"Maybe *I* should give Ronaldinho Spanish lessons."

Now Montse was laughing. "You'd be better qualified, that's for sure."

Later that same day, on the metro, I noticed two construction workers standing in the middle of the carriage, near the doors. Their clothes were flecked with dried cement, and they both wore rugged fawn-colored boots that resembled Timberlands. If I'd been asked to guess where they were from, I would have said Bolivia or Ecuador. Or maybe Peru. One of the men had his eyes closed. Though he was upright, he appeared to be asleep. There was a deep gash between his eyebrows, and as the train pulled into Sants station blood slid in a smooth straight line down one side of his nose. The grinding brakes, the flicker of the lights—the blood... It was like a horror film. And the man didn't react at all. His colleague took out a tissue and wiped the blood away, then stanched the bleeding. The man with the cut didn't even open his eyes. In that moment it came to me. *Unearthly.* That was the word I had been trying to think of earlier, in the café on Plaça Kennedy. That was the word that described the carpenter.

ON A THURSDAY at the beginning of June, Mireia asked if I wanted to go for a drink. At eight o'clock I took the stairs down to the street. The air smelled of jasmine, and the low-voltage yellow glow of the streetlamps made the sky look midnight blue. To the south a half-moon tilted high up in the dark, like the white part in a fingernail. I could easily have caught a bus to the Eixample, but it was such a beautiful evening that I decided to walk.

When I reached the Dalí, Mireia wasn't quite ready to leave—she had to wait for the night manager to arrive—and I sat on a small sofa in the lobby, watching guests come and go. I never minded waiting for Mireia. If anything, I relished it, since I could look forward to the moment when she walked towards me. I would feel privileged, important. I would feel lucky.

We had mojitos at a large, brash place just off Passeig de Gracia, then I took her to Flash Flash for dinner. She had always loved the decor there. The walls were stenciled with life-size black-and-white silhouettes of a Twiggy-lookalike photographer, lights placed where the flashbulb on her camera would be, and the waiters were dressed formally, in white jackets and black bow ties. We ordered tortillas and a bottle of white wine. There was a faint line between Mireia's eyebrows, as if something was bothering her, but when I asked if she was all right she just smiled and blinked.

"Everything's fine," she said.

I insisted on treating her that night. I'd just been paid for a translation. For once, I had some money in the bank.

Later, she suggested we go to a bar near the main square in Born. There was no name and no sign, only a medieval wooden door with hinges as long as my forearm. Set into this large door was a much smaller door that was guarded by an old man in a tuxedo. You walked up to him and asked if you could go inside for a drink, and he said either yes or no. I didn't understand how he arrived at his decisions—I'd been on the wrong end of them several times—but I was never turned away if I was with a woman. Once through the door, you found yourself in a paved courtyard where classical music concerts took place in the summer. The bar itself, which was full of stuffed animals, oil paintings in gilt frames, medieval weapons, Tiffany lamps, and moth-eaten velvet sofas, was like a cross between a junkshop and a museum.

We had been there for about ten minutes when I noticed Vic on the far side of the room. He was sitting with two women in low-cut dresses, and a man who looked like a flamenco dancer, his eyebrows dyed and plucked, his tight black trousers revealing muscular thighs.

"You're not listening," Mireia said.

"Sorry," I said. "I just saw somebody I know."

She glanced over her shoulder. "Who?"

"The man in the shiny suit. He's got his back to us."

At that moment Vic happened to turn sideways to ask the waiter a question, and I watched as something like alarm flashed over Mireia's face.

"I've met that guy before," she said.

"Really?" I said. "Where?"

"At the Dalí. He was a guest."

"A guest? But he lives here. Why would he—?"

"We should leave—" Mireia was already on her feet.

I thought about saying hello to Vic, but something stopped me. He was with glamorous people. I didn't want to show him up. I paid the bill, then hurried after Mireia.

Out on the street I looked one way, then the other, but there was no sign of her.

"The young lady took a taxi."

I glanced round. The gatekeeper was watching me.

"You mean she's gone?"

The old man looked up into the night sky, his lips tightening in a small knowing smile. In his time he must have seen it all.

On the way to Via Laietana I called Mireia.

"I'm sorry, Jordi," she said. "That was a really lovely evening."

"It ended kind of suddenly..." I tried not to sound resentful.

"Seeing that guy upset me."

"Upset you? Why?"

One afternoon she'd fallen into conversation with him, she told me, in the hotel lobby. He seemed pleasant enough. Before they parted, he asked if she would like to come up to his suite for a drink after she finished work. He saw her hesitate, and smiled. It wouldn't just be her, he said. He was having a few people over. She might find it interesting.

"Interesting?" I murmured.

It was a word Vic often used, and he always made it sound like an understatement. It was his way of drawing you in. Bringing you closer.

But Mireia was still talking.

When she walked into the suite that evening, she said, several people were standing around. They were mostly older—in their forties and fifties—and the atmosphere was hushed, expectant. The man who had invited her introduced himself as Brett. He offered her a glass of champagne. She was wearing a strapless sundress. Her shoulders were bare.

Brett turned to the others. "You see? What did I tell you?"

She talked to a Brazilian called Emerson. He had left the top few buttons of his shirt undone, and a number of gold medallions gleamed and shifted in the V-shaped gap. She should come to Castelldefels sometime, he said. He ran a club down there. Next, she met a woman in a Chanel suit who had bad teeth. The woman asked if she had ever acted. Only at school, she said.

A silver-haired man spoke to her next, his mouth close to her ear. "You're *exactly* what we're looking for, my dear."

She had a growing sense of being hemmed in, or even consumed. Finishing her drink, she told Brett she had to go.

He handed her a ring-bound manuscript. "Take this with you."

She asked what it was.

"It's the screenplay for a movie. We'd like you to star in it." He smiled. "This could be your big break."

The title of the movie was THE KEY, which seemed like a reference to all the keys she'd been finding recently. Everything was connected, but not in a good way. She felt dizzy, slightly faint.

"Take it home and read it," Brett said, one hand on her upper arm. "Then you can decide."

She asked how she could contact him, then wished she hadn't, since it conveyed an interest she didn't feel. The question had been prompted by her nervousness, her overwhelming need to leave the room.

"We'll contact you," said the woman with the rotten teeth. "We know where to find you now."

Everyone laughed softly.

Mireia interrupted her story to give directions to her taxi driver.

"His name's not Brett," I said. "It's Vic."

"How do you know?"

"He's my neighbor."

"Maybe Vic isn't his name either."

I thought about that for a moment. A drunk girl knocked into me, then told me to look where I was going.

"I didn't know he made movies," I said. "He never mentioned that."

Mireia gave a little hollow laugh. She told me she was outside her building. She would ring me in a minute.

I reached Via Laietana and waved down a taxi.

On the way back to Sant Gervasi I tried to call Mireia but she didn't answer, and by the time I opened the door to my apartment I was so tired that I went straight to bed and fell asleep.

MY PHONE WAS DEAD when I woke the next morning—I had forgotten to charge it overnight—and it wasn't until after midday that I received Mireia's messages, asking me to come over. That evening, after I finished work, I took the metro to Provença. Mireia answered the door in a black sweater and checked shorts, her legs long and elegant in sheer black tights.

"I hardly slept last night," she said, then turned and moved off into her apartment, leaving me to close the door.

I found her on the sofa in the living room, a lit cigarette held to one side of her mouth. It was already dark, but there were almost no lights on, only two small lamps with crimson shades. I walked over to the window, which looked onto a bricked-over area enclosed on all four sides by the backs of tall apartment buildings. I had always thought it resembled a secret but derelict arena. Sometimes there were stray dogs or cats down there, or sometimes boys kicking a football about. Mireia had told me there was a car park underneath. I liked imagining the rows of silent glinting cars. The petrol-scented gloom.

"There's something I didn't tell you last night," Mireia said.

I looked at her over my shoulder.

"The screenplay he gave me," she said. "It was pornographic."

"Oh." I leaned on the sill, the huge empty space below me, and for a moment I felt I was falling.

"He didn't call it that, of course, your neighbor."

"What did he call it?"

"Art house." That little hollow laugh again. "He said it was a real opportunity for me. Said it could change my life." She stubbed out her cigarette. "He was quite persuasive, actually."

"So you read it, then?"

"Only the first few pages. After that, I felt sick and had to stop."

"Can I see it?"

"I threw it out." She looked at me across the room, her face flushed. "It makes me feel dirty even thinking about it."

I felt a surprising, furtive twinge of lust, which I disguised by asking what part they'd wanted her to play.

"My character is locked in an asylum by mistake," she said. "She gets raped by some of the other inmates—by a doctor too." She lit another cigarette and dragged hard on it. It was as if the experience she was describing had really happened, and she was trying to come to terms with it.

I thought of Vic's business card. Storage Solutions.

"Something else," she said. "As I was leaving, when we were by the door, he asked if he could come round to my apartment. He needed pictures, he said, for his producers. I asked what sort of pictures he was talking about. Nude, he said. He wasn't remotely embarrassed. In fact, I think he even smiled." She flicked some ash into a small glass dish, then shot me a glance. "You didn't give him my address, did you?"

"Why would I do that? I didn't even know you knew each other."

"This guy—he's a friend of yours?" Her voice had sharpened, in disbelief.

"He's not a friend exactly. He just lives in the same building. Sometimes we have coffee." I sat down on the sofa, at the other end from her. "Have you got anything to drink?"

"I want you to do something for me."

I couldn't help noticing she had used the same words Vic had used. "Of course," I said. "What is it?"

"You promise?"

"Yes."

"Next time you see Brett or Vic or whatever the fuck his name is, I want you to tell him to leave me alone." She stood up and smoothed down her shorts. "Is red wine all right?"

THE THOUGHT OF CONFRONTING Vic kept me awake for most of that night. Up until that moment, I hadn't known what to make of his story about the chest of drawers. I didn't believe it, but at the same time I didn't not believe it. Now, though, I began to wonder if he might have intended it as an illustration of the sort of world he inhabited. What if in a roundabout, almost allegorical way he was trying to warn me about himself? At first glance, he might seem open and accessible, someone you could talk to, but he was capable of unexpected and terrifying transformations. As for the carpenter, he wasn't a threat, or even an enigma. He was just an extra, drafted in to give the scene some texture and veracity.

On Monday night I chose not to take the lift to Vic's apartment. In an attempt to delay the dreaded moment, I climbed the stairs instead. Out of breath by the time I reached his floor, I waited on the poorly lit landing until my heart slowed down. At last, I pressed the bell. No one answered. Thank God, I murmured. I was about to retreat towards the stairs when the door opened suddenly and Vic's wife appeared. She was wearing a dressing gown or housecoat made from a pale-pink quilted material, and her face was swollen, as if she'd been asleep. Over her shoulder I saw the chest of drawers, back in its usual place, and was struck once again by the eerie pallor of the wood. I asked if Vic was in. I was a friend, I added. I lived on the third floor.

"He's in London." She blinked slowly, as a cat might. "Can I give him a message?"

"It's all right. It's not urgent." I stepped back, towards the lift. "When will he be home?"

"He didn't say."

I thanked her, then pressed the call button on the lift. Out of the corner of my eye I saw the door begin to close, with Mrs. Drago watching me through the gap.

BY THE MIDDLE OF JUNE I was hard at work on the last few pages of the French novella. The climax took place on a weekday evening. The married couple, Marc and Jeanne, are in the supermarket. As Marc emerges from an aisle, he sees his lover, Sophie, in the dairy section, choosing a yogurt. Backing away, he finds Jeanne and tries to persuade her to return to the car. He says he has a migraine. Can't they do the shopping later, or tomorrow? We're already here, Jeanne says. Let's get it done—and anyway, you don't get migraines. Well, I've got one now, Marc says. Some instinct or intuition tells Jeanne to ignore her husband, and it's not long before she finds out why. As she moves on through the supermarket, she sees Sophie standing at the deli counter. She shouldn't recognize her, of course, but she does. The young woman looks fragile, Jeanne thinks. A bit unstable. And no wonder, when you consider some of the "presents" she has received in recent weeks.

A savage rape story, cut from a tabloid newspaper. A noose. A three-day-old dead rat. Actually, Jeanne is surprised that Sophie hasn't contacted the police. Not that she's bothered by the possibility. She's pretty sure that none of the presents can be traced back to her. She moves towards the deli counter. Perhaps she'll buy some cheese, she thinks, though she knows perfectly well that they don't need any.

She takes up a position next to Sophie, who gives her a quick, uncertain smile. Sophie has no idea who Jeanne is—why would she?—but she does, in that moment, catch a glimpse of Marc, who is lurking near the fruit and vegetables. Marc? she says. Marc walks over. He doesn't say anything to Sophie. He doesn't even look at her. Instead, he takes Jeanne by the arm and steers her towards the checkout. Sophie follows them. She calls his name again—in a soft voice at first, then louder. Someone wants to talk to you, Jeanne says, looking over her shoulder. She's curious to know how the scene will play out. She has never seen her husband and his lover together. She has only imagined it. Sophie blocks their route to the checkout and stares at Marc. How can you be such a monster? she says. Marc doesn't know what Sophie's talking about, but he feels guilty nonetheless. Of behaving badly. Of *something*. You're a monster! Sophie shouts. Jeanne looks at Marc to see how he will respond. He seems paralyzed. Do you two know each other? Jeanne asks. Marc and Sophie both answer at the same time, their words overlapping. Marc says, I've never seen her before. Sophie says, He's been fucking me for months. The word "fucking" lifts clear of the muzak like a shark's fin in calm water, and several shoppers turn their heads. You shit! Sophie tries to slap Marc across the face, but he grabs her wrist. She cries out in pain. Get away from me, he says through gritted teeth. He pushes her hard. Off balance, she topples backwards. The shelf behind her collapses. She sprawls on the floor, surrounded by packets, tins, and jars, some of which have shattered. She has a cut on her hand, and her summer dress is rucked up around her thighs. She looks like what she is—the victim of an assault. Marc stares down at her, hands clenched. A security guard appears. Is there a problem? Jeanne can't take her eyes off her husband. He has never seemed so unsympathetic. So *ugly*. He turns to her. Let's go, he says. No one's going anywhere, says the guard. Sophie sits in a pool of fluid, black olives all around her. She inspects her hand. He hurt me, she tells the guard. He really hurt me. I think I need an ambulance. For God's sake, Marc says. Jeanne steps away, her eyes shifting from Marc to Sophie and back again. What have you been doing? she says to Marc. What have you done? It's as if she has only just realized that he has been having an affair. As if the truth has finally dawned on her. She's behaving how she should have behaved at the start of the book. She is, at last, conventional. She's acting, of course, playing a role, but she feels it so keenly that she doesn't just convince the people who have gathered around them. She convinces herself as well. Now, all of a sudden—*and for the first time*—she becomes a woman who has been deceived, betrayed. Keep away from me, she says to Marc. Stay away. Behind her, in the supermarket car park, blue lights are whirling. Jeanne? Marc says. But she has already turned her back on him. One hand over her mouth, as if she's about to vomit, she hurries out into the night.

I found the ending a little melodramatic—it felt American, somehow, rather than French, and I would have preferred something more ambiguous or slippery—but there was no denying the effectiveness of the prose style. With its clipped, almost abstract quality and its warped logic, it appeared to replicate shortness of breath or panic. Also, I very much liked the way in which the faked discovery of Marc's infidelity at the end of the book ironically mirrored the real discovery at the beginning, and seemed to carry more weight. It was in that moment, I thought, that the morbid and corrupting power of the work found its true expression.

"Did you speak to your friend yet?"

I was having a drink with Mireia, in our usual bar on Santaló. More than two weeks had elapsed since she asked me to have a word with Vic, but I hadn't tried his apartment again, and I'd been avoiding the café on Plaça Kennedy. I told myself I was leaving it to chance. The right moment would present itself. In truth, though, I was putting the whole thing off. I was apprehensive. Scared.

"You haven't," Mireia said, "have you."

I told her I had rung the doorbell, and that Vic's wife had answered. Vic was in London, I said, and she hadn't known when he was coming back. I promised to call on Vic again soon.

Mireia seemed relieved to hear that he had gone away.

"I hope he never comes back," she said.

I didn't tell her that Vic's trips to London were a regular occurrence, and that he would almost certainly be returning in the next few days. He might even have returned already.

She told me she was looking for a new job. She no longer felt comfortable at the Dalí. She couldn't forget what that woman with the rotten teeth had said. She felt she was being watched, even when she was alone in her office. She asked if I thought she was overreacting. Being paranoid. I shook my head. In the circumstances, I said, I would probably feel the same. She had been so unnerved by the whole episode, she told me, so *undermined*, that she had decided to take some holiday. Here, for the first time in our conversation, I thought I detected something less than honest, just the hint of a false note.

"You're going away?" I said.

She nodded.

"Who with?"

She mentioned Flor, a friend of hers. Flor had an aunt who owned a house on Corsica. She was talking faster suddenly, and winding a strand of her long hair round her index finger. The sense that I was being lied to or misled persisted, and the thought that came to me in that moment was a thought I'd often had before. *She's met someone new.* I could hear him in her voice, a presence that was shadowy but urgent.

"I managed to get a flight for this weekend," she hurried on, the words tumbling out. "I'll be gone for several weeks. I just can't wait." She stopped and looked at me, as if an idea had just occurred to her. "You haven't got a guide to Corsica, have you?"

"Why would I have a guide to Corsica?"

She shrugged. "I thought you might have been there."

"No."

I didn't believe she was staying at her friend's aunt's house in Corsica. She probably wasn't even going to Corsica at all. It was just a cover story, to make me feel better. My eyes turned to the window as an ambulance whooped and flashed its way up Santaló. I always felt so bereft when Mireia left the city that I would rather not have known about it. On top of that, I had another reason to be anxious. If she was really going out with someone new, she might use my supposed friendship with Vic as an excuse to see less of me.

"What about you, Jordi?" she said. "Have you got any plans?"

I saw the question for what it was—the feigning of an interest she didn't feel, an attempt to restore the illusion of equality or balance.

"I might go to São Paulo," I said gloomily.

"Really?"

I had wanted her to feel a twinge of jealousy, but she just seemed impressed. I mentioned the party I had been to, and the woman in the red top who had talked about Brazil.

"You're not sleeping with her, are you?"

I laughed. "No."

"Are you sure?" Mireia cocked her head, mischievous, amused. She was pleased with herself for having turned the tables on me. If her hunch was correct, I had a secret too. I was guilty, like her. And I *was* guilty—if only of lying. But it was a pointless and pathetic lie. Why was I claiming to have been inspired by a woman who had bored me half to death?

I finished my drink. "I should be getting home."

"Already?" Mireia looked down at the table. How I longed to lower my face into that tangled mass of hair!

"If I don't see you before you go," I said, "have a great time, won't you."

ABOUT A WEEK LATER, my bell rang at eight o'clock at night, and when I opened the door Vic was standing there in a dark green polo shirt and a pair of gray slacks.

"So this is where you do all that translating," he said.

Before I could say anything, he pushed past me, into the living room. I couldn't remember the last time there had been two people in my apartment. It seemed too many.

Vic was looking around and nodding, his hands in his pockets. "Small, but perfectly formed."

I offered him a beer, which he accepted, then he looked towards the kitchenette, where steam was rising from a pan of boiling water.

"I was about to make spaghetti," I said.

"Turn it off. We're going out."

Ten minutes later, we were in a taxi, heading for El Xalet. It was his favorite restaurant, he told me. He'd had some good news that day. Some very good news. He didn't bother to elaborate. Vic had the irritating habit of withholding information, no matter how trivial that information might be. It was another of his techniques for arousing curiosity. You found yourself asking questions, despite yourself. As the lights of

Plaça d'Espanya swirled past, I wondered how I was going to honor my promise to Mireia. Vic had already insisted that dinner was on him. Things couldn't have been more awkward.

"Shouldn't you be celebrating with your wife?" I said.

Vic laughed loudly, as if my question was the punch-line to a joke. "You obviously don't know Joanna. She hates going out."

I wished I could have changed places with her.

I wished I'd never answered the door.

Once we were seated on the terrace, Vic ordered a bottle of *gran reserva* cava. Perched high on Montjuïc, El Xalet looks north, and the whole city lay before us, a jumble of pink and gray blocks in the warm evening light. Below us, at the foot of the hill, was Federmann's workshop. I thought of the snakeskins rustling on their hooks and shivered, but Vic was leaning back in his chair, relaxed, expansive. He gestured at the view with his champagne glass. "Look at us, Jordi. I mean, where did it all go wrong?"

He laughed again, and this time I laughed with him. I asked him what we were celebrating, and though he still refused to go into any detail he gave me to understand that he had made a great deal of money.

"Was it a business venture?" I asked.

Smiling, he refilled our glasses.

"What about the chest of drawers?" I went on. "Any new developments?"

His smile shrank. "It's all gone quiet." He paused. "Did I tell you I ran into Bill Stone?"

"Is he the guy with the rocking chair?"

Vic nodded. "I asked him if he'd had any trouble with it. He looked at me like I was mental and said it was the best thing he'd ever bought. It changed his life, apparently." Vic blew some air out of his mouth to signify contempt or disbelief, then lit a cigarette. "Maybe I imagined the whole thing. Maybe it was all the drugs I was doing. Lluis is a bad influence." He touched the end of his cigarette against the ashtray. "You remember Lluis? The loft I took you to—that was his."

"What kind of drugs?"

But Vic wouldn't say. Instead, he raised his glass. "Here's to us."

Later, when we had finished our starters and were on our second bottle, he asked what I'd been working on. I began to tell him about the novella, which I had finally delivered a few days earlier, but he was shaking his head before I was even halfway through.

"Women don't behave like that," he said.

"This one does." I kept my voice light. "It takes all sorts to make a world."

The look Vic gave me was affectionate but condescending. "And there was me, thinking you knew about people."

I drank from my water glass.

"Vic," I said, "there's something I have to tell you."

He looked up, his head turned a fraction to one side, but both his eyes on mine.

"You have to stay away from Mireia," I said.

"Mireia? Who's Mireia?" He reached for a bread roll.

"My girlfriend. Mireia."

Vic was tearing pieces off the roll and tossing them in his mouth, then chewing hungrily.

"You approached her in the Hotel Dalí, where she works," I went on. "You invited her up to your room for a drink—"

"My suite. It was a suite."

"You asked her if she wanted to be in a film."

"Any law against that?"

"You used a false name. You called yourself Brett."

Vic threw the remains of the bread roll on the table. "Look, Jordi, I'm not like you, sitting in some crappy little apartment all day, tapping away on a laptop. I know a lot of people. I see a lot of people. I 'approach' people, as you put it, all the fucking time."

My cheeks had flushed. I looked down at my empty plate.

"I take you out for dinner and this is the thanks I get. Christ." Vic stared out across the terrace. The lower half of his face was twisted, as if he had bitten into something sour.

Just then, I saw right through him, a moment of perceptiveness or clarity that lifted me out of the predicament in which I found myself. This was what people like Vic Drago did. They opened up new worlds, they treated you to things you weren't accustomed to and hadn't asked for, things they insisted on, and then, when you were clearly in their debt, they began to exact a kind of payment. And you had no choice but to go along with it. You had to take the rough because you'd already taken the smooth. But I was determined not to be deflected from the task I had been assigned. What was the worst that could happen? My friendship with Vic would end, and I would have to find a different café to go to in the mornings.

"All I did was ask you to leave her alone," I said. "It's not exactly complicated. She doesn't want to be in a film—especially a film like that."

"A film like what?"

I didn't answer. I didn't feel I had to.

Vic's laugh had an edge of malice to it now. "Your girlfriend—if that's what she is, which I seriously doubt—didn't have to come up to my suite for a drink, did she? She could've said no."

"It's not that. It's—"

"It's what? What is it, Jordi?" He stressed my name, as if it was not a name at all, but an expletive.

My mouth was dry, and I wished I could finish the cava in my glass. I didn't want to touch it, though, because he'd already told me he was paying.

"There I am, trying to do someone a favor, and suddenly it's like, *Stay away.*" He leaned back and folded his napkin, and when he looked at me again his face was hard and cold. As on the evening of his drinks party, I sensed something cavalier in him, a refusal to recognize borders or limits, a willingness to ride roughshod over things he had no time for. "Let me tell you what I see," he said. "I see a spoiled bitch who thinks a bit too highly of herself. She's got looks and charm, but underneath she's frightened. And then there's you." He poured himself some more cava and downed it in one, grimacing as if the wine was corked. "You know what you are, don't you. You don't need me to tell you that." He put his glass on the table. "Well, I'm going to tell you anyway. You're worse than frightened. You're a mouse."

I had thought I would be impervious to anything that he might say—I had thought I was prepared—but I had tears in my eyes. Embarrassed and ashamed, I couldn't meet his gaze.

"A fucking mouse is what you are. *Stay away from my girlfriend.*" He let out another harsh mocking laugh. "Who's going to make me? You?" He pushed his chair back and stood up, then dropped his napkin on the table. "You and whose army?"

"And you?" I said quietly, not looking up. "What are you, then?"

He opened his wallet and threw a twenty-euro note on the table. "That's for your cab home."

I watched him walk away, his shoulders square, his footsteps abrupt, decisive. The waiters nodded and smiled as he swept past. If the world had been asked to choose between us, it was clear which one it would have sided with. I went on sitting there, staring at the view, and when I finally felt ready to leave, some ten minutes later, I left his money on the table.

I DIDN'T GO TO SÃO PAULO—or anywhere else for that matter—but Mireia's decision to take a long holiday followed by my humiliating night with Vic marked a turning point in my life. In early September, around the time of the *Diada Nacional,* I met my old university professor in a noisy, unpretentious place off Gran de Gracia. In his mid-fifties, with sad eyes and a neatly trimmed mustache and beard, Jaume vaguely resembled Umberto Eco, but he dressed in a style I thought of as English—corduroy trousers, tweed jackets with leather patches on the elbows, stout brogues. We saw each other two or three times a year, and always ended up drinking too much.

"Still obsessed with the beautiful Mireia?" he said as he joined me at the bar.

I smiled. "Naturally."

Jaume shook his head. "You're onto a hiding to nothing there, I'm afraid."

"You're hardly the first person to tell me that."

"I'm sure I'm not."

"The thing is," I said, "of all the hidings to nothing I have known, she's the best."

Jaume laughed.

I asked after his wife, Montse.

"You know Montse," he said. "Never a dull moment." He ran one hand across his thinning hair. "We've got Amy staying with us at the moment. She's English. Maybe you know her?"

"I don't think so."

"She's facing a murder charge."

I stared at Jaume. "What?"

"She killed a man in Sarrià—at least, that's what she's accused of."

I was still staring. I thought I'd heard about the case. Something to do with an old-age pensioner and an illegal immigrant.

"Montse says the whole thing was an accident." Jaume shook his head again, then drained his glass of wine. "By the way, she's very happy with the job you did on that novella."

We switched to our favorite subject—the current state of fiction on the Iberian peninsula—and it was only towards midnight that Jaume suddenly remembered why he had suggested that we meet. A well-known British publisher was looking for an editor who could acquire new French and Spanish authors, he told me, and he had taken the liberty of mentioning my name. In that moment, the whole room shifted, as though it had been hoisted on a crane, and Jaume's next words reached me only faintly, as if across a great distance.

"Of course, it would mean moving to London," he said. "I hope I did the right thing. It's just that you seemed the perfect person for the job..."

London, I thought.

I saw Camden Town in the winter. Bare trees, a dull gray sky. White stucco-fronted houses with black railings. I saw a pub on the canal. Live bands most nights, a funny, foul-mouthed Irish woman behind the bar. The smell of beer and roll-ups. I remembered how free I'd felt, even though I'd had no money.

"Jordi?" Jaume was giving me a searching look.

"Sorry," I said. "Who should I contact?"

The following weekend I took a bus to my mother's house near the Parc de l'Oreneta. After my father's death in the late nineties, I started visiting my mother every week, but I hadn't seen much of her during the summer, and felt I should make it up to her. I arrived with a bunch of orange roses and a painted wooden box I had found in a gift shop in Sarrià. My mother had made lunch—cold roast chicken, a green salad, and *patatas bravas* from Bar Tomás. Their garlic mayonnaise and chili sauce was the best in the city, and their *patatas bravas* had been a favorite of mine ever since I was a child.

"We're going to stink," I said.

I reminded my mother of the time I took a girl to Bar Tomás on a date. She was called Estel. I ordered the *patatas bravas,* as always, but Estel ordered croquettes, and when I tried to kiss her she recoiled. I never saw her again.

My mother smiled, then reached for her wine. "You know, I've been wanting to talk to you—about Mireia..."

I rolled my eyes. "Again?"

"I've been thinking that maybe, in the past, I was a little hard on her."

"That's ironic," I said, "because just recently I've had the feeling that you might have been right all along." I broke off, surprised at myself. I had been thinking out loud—I wasn't aware of having had any such feeling—but it seemed truer than anything I had said in ages. "It's time I stopped living in the hope that something might happen," I went on. "We don't belong together. Perhaps we never did."

"If she's what you want, Jordi, you should fight for her."

But my mother's change of heart had come too late—or rather, she was addressing a version of myself that I'd already left behind.

"I've been waiting for Mireia for years," I said, "and I can't wait any longer." I hesitated, unsure if I should tell her. Then I plunged ahead. "I've applied for a job in England."

We spent the rest of the afternoon talking about London, and though my mother was sad that I would no longer be close by—I was her only child—she told me that this new challenge was exactly what I needed.

"And I can always come and visit," she added, her eyes bright suddenly, with tears.

"Of course you can," I said, taking her hand. "Whenever you like."

I WENT TO SEE MIREIA two days after she returned from Corsica. If she had been with a new man, she was careful not to mention it—or perhaps, in my jealousy, I had imagined the whole thing, and she had traveled with a girlfriend after all. Either way, it was doing me no good. While she was away, I had flown to London to meet the publishers Jaume had told me about, and they had taken me to lunch after the interview and offered me the job. I would be starting in October.

I stood with my back to the window in Mireia's living room. After several weeks on the beach, she was like a hyper-real version of herself, her eyes greener than I remembered, her hair streaked with blond. She had never looked more beautiful. That only served to strengthen my resolve, and I decided to tell her I was leaving Barcelona. She wasn't happy for me. On the contrary. She seemed bewildered, almost outraged, as if I was trying to damage her.

"This is all so sudden," she kept saying.

I had been living hand to mouth for years, I told her, making a few thousand here, a few thousand there. I had been longing for my life to change, but I had done nothing to bring that change about. I didn't say that I had been waiting for her. I didn't say that I had finally realized that she didn't want a relationship with me, and never would, and that all I could expect from her was frustration and disappointment.

She sank down on to her sofa. "God, my head is *spinning*."

I experienced a burst of malicious satisfaction, and Jeanne, the narrator of *Giving*, came to mind. Vic had been wrong to think the story wasn't realistic.

"By the way," I said, turning to the window, "I did what you asked. I told Vic to leave you alone."

As I stared at the huge bricked-over area, which was deserted that evening, I thought I felt Mireia stiffen behind me.

"My neighbor," I said, "remember?"

I gave her an abbreviated version of what had happened on the terrace at El Xalet. He had walked out, I told her, and I hadn't seen him since.

"You know, in the end," I said, "I don't think it was as big a deal as you were making out."

"What do you mean?"

"Maybe he just fancied you. Maybe that whole business with the movie was him trying to impress you."

Even as I spoke, I felt this objective tone was a departure for me, a by-product or indication of the new freedom I'd attained, and Mireia noticed.

"You almost sound as if you're on his side," she said.

I glanced at her over my shoulder. "I did what you asked. I can't do any more than that."

"No, of course not." She looked down at her hands.

I was about to say something more conciliatory, but she spoke first.

"I slept with him."

"*What?*"

"I slept with him. Your neighbor." She paused. "It only happened once."

I stared at the bricked-over area. The whole world tilted, and I felt sick. When I spoke, I felt my voice coming from somewhere else. Somewhere outside me.

"But you said you were frightened of him. You said—"

"That was after." She sighed. "The drink I had with those people in his room was after."

"So why did he need the photos? He'd already seen you."

"I don't know. To show the others?"

I turned and looked at her again. There was defiance on her face, but there was also shame.

"I'm sorry, Jordi," she said. "I should have told you."

I picked up my jacket and started for the door.

"Don't go. Please."

I didn't have anything to do that evening, but I had to get away from her. I needed time to think. Or not think. But she had followed me across the room.

She placed a hand on my arm, her face close to mine. "Don't hold it against me."

"I've been an idiot."

"You've always been such a good friend to me—"

"*Friend.*" The word caught in my throat.

I left her apartment, not bothering to close the door.

Out on the street, the traffic was too loud, and the sky, though cloudy, was too bright. I stood on the pavement, with people pushing past me. I had the brief but vivid sensation that I had just been released from an institution where I'd been held for years, and was overwhelmed by the nonchalant speed and thrust of the world in which I found myself, a world that was now completely unfamiliar to me.

BEFORE I FLEW TO LONDON, I met Mireia in a café in Barceloneta. She had been for an interview at the W, a new five-star hotel that had been built on the waterfront. She told me it had gone well, though she wasn't sure she would get the job. My eyes moved beyond her. The hotel stood out against the blue sky like a sail made of mirror glass.

She reached into her bag and took out a bunch of keys. "I found these the other day, in Sant Andreu."

I picked up the keys and studied them. The key ring they were attached to was a square of silver metal with a suspension bridge etched into it. Underneath, in black, was the name of an English city: BRISTOL.

"I don't think it means anything," Mireia said, "do you?"

"No." I pushed the keys back across the table.

Later, she asked when I was leaving.

"Friday," I said.

"So soon?" She reached behind her head and lifted her hair away from her neck, then let it drop, tumbling, against her back. Didn't she realize that she could make my heart ache with the simplest of gestures? "Can I visit you?"

I smiled. "That's what my mother said."

"London..." She gave me a reproachful look. "You'll probably go and marry one of those English girls."

"Probably," I said lightly. "But I'll always love you."

THE NEXT DAY, as I stood in my apartment, surrounded by cardboard boxes, I remembered something Vic had said. *Small, but perfectly formed.* Even at the time, the comment had sounded suggestive. Knowing what I now knew, I found it sickening. I hadn't seen him since that night, not even from a distance. I had stopped going to the café on Plaça Kennedy, and when I left my building I always took the stairs, since I didn't want to risk running into him in the lift. If my doorbell rang unexpectedly, I pretended to be out. But as my departure date approached I began to think it would be cowardly to leave without saying goodbye. I felt the need to clear the air.

At seven o'clock on Wednesday evening, I left my apartment and stepped into the waiting lift. As usual, the cramped space smelled of other people's sweat. I thought I could also smell Vic's cologne, as if he'd been standing where I was standing only moments earlier. My stomach knotted, but I forced myself to press the button that said SOBREATICO.

The lift jolted to a halt on the ninth floor, and when I stepped out onto the narrow landing I noticed that the door to Vic's apartment was ajar. I moved closer, the silence broken only by the chatter of a helicopter overhead.

I pushed on the door. The gap widened.

"Vic?"

His hallway seemed emptier than I remembered, though the chest of drawers was still there.

"Vic? It's Jordi."

My voice sounded strangled, weak. I cleared my throat.

Then I heard footsteps approaching from the living room, and a young blond woman appeared. She had a phone in one hand and a glossy folder in the other.

"Senyor Carbonell?"

"No," I said.

"But you've come to see the apartment?"

I shook my head. "Actually, I was looking for Vic Drago."

"Ah yes," she said. "The previous tenant."

"Has he moved out?"

The woman held my gaze. "So far as we can tell, he left about a week ago."

"And his wife?"

"His wife too."

I looked beyond the woman and saw that the living room had been cleared of all its furniture, though there were still some plants on the terrace.

"I didn't know," I said.

The woman indicated the chest of drawers. "He seems to have left this behind, but we rent the apartment unfurnished. I don't suppose you want it?"

"No!"

I had answered so abruptly and with such vehemence that I startled her, and she seemed suspicious suddenly, as if I might be implicated in Vic's disappearance, or at least more involved than I was letting on.

"No," I said again, more gently. "Thank you. But I'm about to move myself—to London."

The woman's eyes returned to the chest of drawers. "It's unusual, don't you think?"

"That he left it behind, you mean?"

"Well, yes. But also it's not like any chest of drawers I've ever seen."

"It's made out of birch wood."

"Really?"

I nodded. "From Siberia."

She gave me an uncertain look, as if she thought I might be pulling her leg.

"That's what Vic Drago told me, anyway," I went on. "He told me a lot of things, and they weren't all true."

In that moment the lift jolted in its shaft and began to grind its way down through the building.

"That's probably your client." I stepped out onto the landing, then I turned back. "You don't happen to know where Senyor Drago went, do you?"

"I was about to ask you the same thing," she said. "You're not the only person looking for him."

"I see. Well, sorry I can't help."

"Good luck with your move."

"Thank you."

Rather than wait for the lift, I set off down the stairs. When my head was almost on a level with the floor, I glanced back towards Vic's apartment. Through the half-open door I saw the estate agent approach the chest of drawers, then bend from the waist and run a hand down one of its sturdy legs.

IT SEEMED OBVIOUS that Vic Drago would crop up again at some point in my life, and I felt that my move to London, his hometown, only increased the chances of that happening, but the months went by and he failed to appear. Sometimes I thought I caught a glimpse of him—on a tube platform, in the lobby of a cinema—and I would rush over. *Vic?* But it was always a stranger. It turned out that there were a lot of men who looked like him. Not just in London. Everywhere. Sometimes he would stroll square-shouldered through my dreams, dressed in one of his loud jackets and smelling like a casino, his presence freighted with a significance I could never quite determine. Every once in a while, I would Google him—*vic drago storage, vic drago barcelona, vic drago embezzlement, vic drago pornography*, and even *vic drago interpol*—but none of the results I pulled up bore any resemblance to the man I'd known. Perhaps Mireia had been right after all, and Vic was a pseudonym. Like Brett.

Once, on my way to a wedding in Buckinghamshire, I drove along a section of the North Circular, making for the M1. On a whim, I left the main road at Staples Corner and found myself in an industrial estate, exactly the kind of place where I'd imagined Vic's warehouses would be. I could picture him on those characterless streets, stepping out of his black Lexus, his gold chain bracelet glinting on his wrist. *You've got to show up now and then. Keep the bastards on their toes.* I spent the next twenty minutes driving round the area. There were plenty of warehouses—some even offered storage—but I didn't see the name VIC DRAGO anywhere. Of course he might have sold up by now. He might be running a different business entirely. It was all too long ago, too far away.

Someone did appear, though—in the end...

I was walking east along Piccadilly on a sunlit afternoon in late March when a man in a long dark coat emerged from a doorway. The wavy black hair, streaked with gray. Something intense about the gaze. I knew I had seen him before, but it took me a few moments to recall his name, and he was almost past me by the time I spoke.

"Daniel Federmann?"

He stopped in midstride.

"I thought it was you," I said. "Amazing."

His head turned, and his eyes moved across my face, impassive. "Do we know each other?"

"I came to your workshop once, in Barcelona."

He said he had no recollection of me. "I'm sorry," he added. "That sounds rude."

I laughed. "It's all right. I mean, think of all the people who must have walked into your shop."

He looked down at the pavement.

"It was several years ago," I went on, "but I've never forgotten the quality of your work—the craftsmanship..."

"Thank you," he said.

Unwilling to let him go as yet, I searched for a question. What was he doing in London? Visiting museums, he told me. I asked which ones. He mentioned Sir John Soane's and Leighton House. He'd been indulging his interest in furniture, he said. He smiled ruefully, as if he had admitted to an embarrassing pastime or condition.

"Did you ever see Vic Drago again?"

Just then, I thought I saw two expressions on Federmann's face, one inquiring, or even wary, the second arriving a fraction of a second later, and sliding over it, concealing it, and I was left looking at a man who appeared to be calmly dredging his memory for a name.

"Vic Drago," I said. "He bought a chest of drawers from you."

If I had caught Federmann off guard, there was no sign of it now. He was watching me carefully, as if I was telling him something he didn't know.

"It was made of birch wood, from Siberia." I had the feeling I was talking in code, but I kept going. "The wood was cut by the light of a full moon. That's what gave it its special pliancy. Its pale color."

Federmann's smile had returned. "I used to say a lot of things to make a sale."

"It wasn't true?"

"No."

"But you remember the piece?"

He nodded.

"And Drago?" I said. "You remember him too?"

"I think I know who you mean. Was he a friend of yours?"

"He was my neighbor."

Federmann glanced across the road at Fortnum & Mason's, with its eau-de-nil window frames and its oversize clock. "He killed himself, didn't he? Or was it an accident?"

Though we were standing in spring sunlight, a chill shook me. "Is he dead?"

"I believe so." Federmann paused. "I'm not sure of the facts," he said. "I read about it, I think—in a newspaper."

"Do you remember how he died?"

"I'm afraid not." Federmann pulled his coat around himself, as if he also suddenly felt cold. "Sorry, but I really should be going."

"Daniel," I said. "That's an angel's name, isn't it."

He looked at me, and there was nothing on his face, nothing except a faint glimmer of amusement. Then we shook hands and parted.

When I had walked a few paces, I stopped and glanced over my shoulder, and I was surprised to see that Federmann had done the same. Our eyes met across a distance, as they had once before, in his workshop at the foot of Montjuïc. At that moment, I had the sense that I had been looking in the wrong place, that it wasn't Vic Drago I should have been thinking about but Federmann, it was Federmann I should have been thinking about all along, but he had already turned away, and I had no choice but to turn away myself, and we moved off in opposite directions, along paths that would never cross again.